S. D. PERRY

VIRUS

Based on the Motion Picture Screenplay by
Chuck Pfarrer and Dennis Feldman
Based on the Dark Horse Comic Book
Series "Virus" Created by Chuck Pfarrer

TOR®

A TOM DOHERTY ASSOCIATES BOOK
NEW YORK

.As always, Mÿk, who takes care of me very well.
And for Sera, who loves the movies.

VIRUS

A Tor Book
Published by Tom Doherty Associates, Inc.
175 Fifth Avenue
New York, NY 10010

Tor Books on the World Wide Web:
http://www.tor.com

Tor® is a registered trademark of Tom Doherty Associates, Inc.

ISBN: 0-812-54158-8

First Tor edition: August 1998

Printed in the United States of America

0 9 8 7 6 5 4 3 2 1

• Introduction •

Virus is a science fiction story. And science fiction stories are best when based closely on facts or possibilities. How well these type of stories work is in how well they can blur the line between fact and fiction.

My first "literary" introduction to science fiction was the book, *2001: A Space Odyssey*. I grew up in the late Fifties in northern California, during the heyday of science fiction and horror B movies. I loved those movies. Aliens would come to Earth outside a small town and terrorize the residents, possessing them, torturing them. I must confess that at that time, I was not a great reader of books. The books I received the most enjoyment from were comic books, which I had to hide from my parents, who greatly disapproved of them.

In the novel *2001,* the Monolith was a teacher, sent by alien caretakers responsible for the success of life in our solar system. If the protohumans in the beginning of the story survived on Earth, they would prosper, eventually discovering another Monolith on the moon. Neat idea. In the film *2001,* none of this was explained. But because I had read the book, I understood all of it—the harmony of novel and film working together to immerse me in the total story. This type of book had value to me. "You've read the book, now see the movie" suddenly made sense. The only danger would be if the movie didn't live up to my own expectations of the book.

On September 20, 1995, I dove 12,378 feet to the final resting place of the RMS *Titanic*. Two and a half miles beneath the surface of the North Atlantic, one of thirty-five people to have ever done so.

I was in a twenty-two-foot orange-and-white Russian submersible called *Mir II*. James Cameron was in *Mir I*. It was his dive and his expedition and it was at his pleasure that I was there. I was part of the crew that was filming what would later become the opening sequence of the movie *Titanic*.

The 1995 expedition spent thirty-one days in the North Atlantic, 600 plus miles south-southeast of Saint John's, Newfoundland. We were for two weeks stationed above the *Titanic*.

Our home away from home for those weeks was the Russian research vessel *Akademik Mstislav Keldysh* out of Kaliningrad. Gleaming white, her only other colors were the dark green of her upper decks and the bright orange of her two seventy-man lifeboats. At 450 feet, *Keldysh* was the largest vessel of her kind in the world and the pride of the Shirshov Oceanographic Institute. She carried a crew of 130, had eighteen science labs, complete machine shops, and was a totally self-contained floating condominium complex. A city of Russians with a few Canadians and Americans thrown into the mix.

During those four long weeks, the crew of the *Keldysh* launched and recovered the *Mir I* and *Mir II* submersibles twelve times, did oceanographic studies (plus atmospheric tests, involving the Mir space station as it passed overhead), aided a ship at sea, and experienced two hurricanes on site: Hurricanes Louis and Marilyn. Louis being the most memorable, with forty-foot seas and ninety-knot winds. A kickass storm that seemed to go on forever. An experience I would never forget.

What does this have to do with *Virus*? Everything.

A month earlier I had been given a script by Universal to consider directing. It was based on the Dark Horse graphic novel created by Chuck Pfarrer. Mike Richardson from Dark Horse was an old friend. The producer would be Gale Anne Hurd, also a good friend. Gale had produced *The Abyss*, whose visual effects I had supervised. I was intrigued by this idea, but at the time I was already set to supervise the visual effects on *Titanic*. I was just awaiting word of a start date. If *Virus* was real, I would have to choose between supervising visual effects on *Titanic* and directing a major studio picture.

But at that point, I wasn't completely satisfied with the story of *Virus*. It was a very dense and complicated story involving a state-of-the-art Chinese spy ship and lots of grotesquely modified humans. The concept didn't excite me at first. The Chinese had no such ships. Only the Russians and Americans did. The studio wanted an answer.

I received word the next day from Lightstorm. I was to be on a plane headed for Halifax that coming weekend. I would be part of the 1995 *Titanic* expedition, but under one condition—I couldn't tell a soul. Not the studio, not Gale Hurd—no one.

We were two weeks at sea before Jim brought *Virus* up in casual conversation. He had talked to Gale before we left Halifax and he wanted to know if I had made up my mind about doing it. I hadn't. I told him I wasn't happy with the story.

Jim's advice to me was make *Virus* my own. Bring my real-life experiences to it. Be a director. Directing a major motion picture was a gift and should be taken seriously. He was kicking me out of the nest.

The following weeks I thought hard about it. After all, half of my relatives were fishermen. The crew of *Virus* could be a compilation of the numerous people I had crossed paths with over the years. The tug crew I had worked with in the Northern Pacific, on *The Abyss*, could be assimilated into the story along with the Russians of the *Keldysh* crew. And there was the *Keldysh* itself.

Hell, the whole story could take place in a hurricane.

Between dive operations I took copious notes. Upon our return Dennis Feldman (*Species*) was hired to help me create the story that I wanted to tell. That was the fun part of the process. Directing it would be a more difficult path. Reality would collide with concept. The budget, locations, time, and people would influence the grand scheme of things and—in the final completed harsh reality of film—pace.

In the editing process pace and performance are the key to a successful film. Sometimes your favorite scenes end up on the cutting room floor in order to enhance the flow of the narrative. It's part of the creative struggle between art and commerce. Time is money.

But that is not the case with the written word. It will always be there, the way you always imagined it. As many words as you want.

The film was completed by the time I read the final novelization of *Virus*. I was ecstatic. Here was the story as I had always imagined it. Through all the various drafts of the screenplays. A seafaring tale with all the ideas (all the best ideas) completed as a continuous story, right there on the page. I could take my time to savor the moments. Taste them. I could spend time with Foster, Steve, or the Captain at my own pace. Have another cup of coffee if I wanted. That is why I'm so happy with the way Danelle Perry finished the story, expanding on the original idea. Filling in the gaps. She made it her own. The way I hoped it would be.

John Bruno
Director, *Virus*, 1998

O friend, never strike sail to a fear! Come into port greatly,
or sail with God the seas.
—Ralph Waldo Emerson

▪ Prologue ▪

It was just past dawn and the ocean was calm and smooth beneath the *Volkov,* the South Pacific waters lapping gently against the metal hull. It was typhoon season, but uneasy seas were a hundred miles away; the giant vessel carefully held its lonely position in the brilliant early light, gleaming white upon a vast blanket of deep and quiet blue.

The second of the three parabolic dish antennas that dominated her main deck rotated skyward, the hum of machinery at work lost to the gentle winds high above. It was a magnificent ship and a glorious day, the kind of day that made one long to lounge in the sun and breathe in the salt, read a book, perhaps take a nap in the open air . . .

Dr. Nadia Vinogradova scowled at the pleasant images, wishing that she could do these things and vaguely irritated that there was not a chance in hell; as it was, the day that she had scheduled probably wouldn't allow her to set foot outside until well after dark. She generally enjoyed her job, but early morning was not her best time; Alexi was fond of telling her that she was a pouty little girl until noon, and she had to admit (at least to herself, anyway) that he was right.

Nadia sighed inwardly and focused her attention on the task at hand; it was time. The overly bright C deck communications room was stuffy and she felt a little crowded by the men that sat with her at the video console—but she could also feel their anticipation and was proud to lead such an eager team.

She tapped a few keys and cleared her throat, facing the monitor. As always, she felt a small thrill when contacting the station; she'd worked long and hard to make senior science officer, years of proving herself to be coolly competent and worthy of respect—but she was also still secretly delighted by this aspect of her position. It never failed to impress upon her the importance of her work.

"MIR Station, MIR Station, this is the Akademic Research Vessel *Vladislav Volkov*. Do you read, over?"

She looked up at the screen and into the pleasantly squinting face of Colonel Kominski. He was wearing a Houston Rockets T-shirt, a wellworn gift from one of the American astronauts, and looked as tired as she felt.

"Loud and clear, *Volkov*. Nadia, is that you? Over."

Nadia smiled. "Good morning, Colonel. Is your disk array in position?"

"That depends. It's early yet, I haven't had my tea."

Nadia heard Alexi chuckle behind her; the captain of the *Volkov* was a notorious tea drinker, always a cup in hand.

Nadia rolled her eyes, still smiling. "Very funny, Colonel. Your data, please?"

The cosmonaut reached overhead and flipped switches, then sighed dramatically in mock resignation. "Finalizing coordinates as we speak; preparing for data downlink in—thirty seconds."

He pointed to his second-in-command, Captain Lonya Rostov, who tapped at another switch on his console. "Yes, sir."

Nadia grinned at the two cosmonauts, 150 miles above the *Volkov* in the core module of the MIR. The data about to be sent was of particular interest to her, the first of a series of tests on cell factories performed in Kvant 1; she looked forward to studying the results and adding to her research on bioprocesses.

But right now . . .

"Lonya?" she asked sweetly.

The captain arched his eyebrows. "Yes, Nadia?"

"Bishop to king six."

Lonya Rostov frowned and looked up at the chessboard mounted over his console, studying it intently. Nadia had to suppress an urge to gloat; it was a strong move and she could tell that he hadn't considered it.

Put that in your belly, Rostov! He wasn't going to win this one.

Behind the frowning captain, Nadia saw one of the visiting female cosmonauts at an observation port—Kostoev, Nadia thought, but she couldn't remember the woman's first name. Ludmila? She held a camera and had raised it suddenly to take a picture of whatever she saw.

Colonel Kominski interrupted Rostov's chess musings abruptly. "We are twenty seconds from downlink corridor. Mark . . ."

Rostov sighed and took it up. "Mark. Starting automatic sequencing now . . . eighteen . . . seventeen . . ."

The woman, Kostoev, broke in urgently, her voice high and anxious. "Lonya, out your starboard portal—something is coming straight at us."

Rostov stopped the verbal count and turned, peered at something offscreen. Nadia saw something like fear pass over his even features and felt her own muscles tense—Lonya Rostov was not an easily frightened man.

"What is that? Colonel, you'd better look at this. Something's approaching and we just got in its way—"

Nadia waited, suddenly filled with a deep sense of foreboding. "Something" approaching? Though highly improbable, perhaps a meteor, an unscheduled shuttle—but what could be headed for the MIR that Rostov wouldn't know?

Alarmed, she leaned closer to the monitor, watching carefully—and although she had a clear view, the next few seconds were a confused blur of motion and sound.

There was a crackle of sharp static and the screen flashed a vivid blue, overlaying the interior of the module in a lightning-fast series of brilliant shocks. The cosmonauts were suddenly outlined by what looked like giant bolts of electricity, arcing and snapping through the air. There was an eerie, high-pitched electronic squeal like nothing Nadia had ever heard—

—and the picture on her console distorted and turned to dark snow. Over the blaring static, Nadia clearly heard screams and shouts of mortal terror.

Horrified and bewildered, Nadia punched at the relay keys, her heart pounding. And then everything went out, the screams cut off abruptly as the monitor died.

"MIR Station? MIR Station—?"

Only silence and a blank screen; nothing.

Nadia turned to the captain, met his stunned gaze with her own. "Alexi, all audio and visual links are gone, something is very wrong—"

The transmission!

Nadia looked back at her console, at the smaller screen set next to the video receiver. The numbers flashed, green against black, and suddenly she wanted to scream, unreasonably frightened as the MIR completed the countdown.

3...2...1...

The soft beep from the machine seemed incredibly loud in the shocked silence of the room. Nothing happened, and Nadia looked back at Alexi, opened her mouth to say something, ask him what to do—

—when a strange and terrible light erupted into the control room.

Huge, blue electrical arcs snapped across the chamber, crackling with power and heat. Nadia leapt to her feet, saw and heard the other crew members do the same, shouting and stumbling to get away from the surging bolts of brilliant light.

Nadia spun, searched wildly for the source of the energy, terrified—and stopped, stared at the console computer screens in the chaos of the invading radiance.

Information scrolled across the monitors so rapidly that she could hardly make any of it out. Numbers, lines of flashing icons, layout prints, and pages upon pages of stored data whipped up and were gone as she watched, frozen in disbelief.

What—

A string of letters and numbers suddenly appeared alone on one screen, followed by another and then a third. Nadia's mouth went dry as she realized what they were.

"Captain, someone's accessing the main computer!"

Alexi followed her wide-eyed gaze, stared at the monitor in pure astonishment. "Impossible! I'm the only one who knows the access code—"

There was a jolting flash of blue light and they were both knocked to the floor. Static screamed from everywhere and the electronic squeal that she'd heard from the MIR filled the room, shrill and insane. Papers and readouts flew through the air.

"Shut the power off!" Alexi screamed.

Nadia looked up, saw her research immunologist still on his feet. "Shut it down! Shut it all down!"

She saw the terror on Yandiev's face, but he didn't hesitate. The scientist lunged for the power switch—

—and Nadia saw a bolt of the crackling blue light strike him, rip through his chest like an electrical sword. The brilliance seared his flesh, enveloped him, and Nadia screamed then, all semblance of control, of rational thought, torn away.

Anatoly Yandiev had burst into flame, every part of his staggering body consumed by raging fire. He crumpled, burning, to the deck.

Nadia was still screaming as everything swirled away, that horrible high-pitched sound chasing her into a blackness that crackled and spat with a dark and unknown purpose.

Seven hundred forty nautical miles south of Fiji, Leiah had grown from a petulant child into a serious bitch in a matter of hours—an insane, terrible, class four screamer that had churned the seas into forty-plus-foot swells, raging beneath an ominous, boiling night sky.

Kelly Foster sat on the heaving, humid bridge of the *Sea Star* and studied the typhoon, pulsing spirals of innocuous-looking light on the radar when it wasn't obscured by surges of violent static. The tug rocked wildly, thrown into the storming night on heaving waters and plunged back down into deep valleys of ocean. Foster was scared, and more than a little pissed off.

She'd warned Everton as soon as the system had organized into a tropical depression; he'd had hours, listening to her increasingly urgent reports of convections on the rise. Had he heard any of it, let her change course to give the storm a safely wide berth? "We'll clear it, she won't turn, I *know* these waters," he'd said.

The typhoon had made the upgrade to light magenta at just after 0300, and by the looks of it, Leiah would hit white before she was through.

And here we are in the midst, here I am like a goddamn fool on a ship run by an even bigger fool. What the hell was I thinking, signing up for this?

The ship bucked and moaned against the turbulent waters and Foster winced as another giant wave crashed against their tow. The heavy container barge was going to drag them down, *if* the aft winch actually held out, and the captain still wouldn't listen to reason. He'd let their options run out with each decision put off, and now they were all going to pay for it.

Foster gritted her teeth against rising anger and turned to the man who paced the deck behind her, chewing nervously on his damned peanuts. Captain Everton had stalked back and forth for over an hour, wearing his battered wool hat, a 6 shot strapped to one hip like some mad, grizzled sailor from an ancient movie.

Just call me Ishmael, she thought sourly.

"Winds gusting to one-ten," she said. "If it gets to one-thirty, we're on the verge of a category five."

Everton didn't answer, walked past her to stare through the bridge's aft window, searching for his precious cargo in the driving darkness. He bellowed to the third member of their little bridge party as if the helmsman were deaf, his voice rough and powerful.

"Put 'er back into the wind, Woods! Forty-five degrees down-swell!"

J. W. Woods, Jr., spun the wheel tightly, coffee cup in one hand, his face stretched taut and shiny with sweat. The lanky blond helmsman still wore a fading black eye from his last bar fight and looked unhappy but loyally determined, always eager to prove his worth; Woods was the only crew member who truly seemed to enjoy kissing Everton's ass. The man was a toadying creep, pure and simple, and she could expect no help there. Steve, Squeaky, and the other two hands probably had more sense, but they were busy below—and not too likely to side with her about anything, the way they'd ignored her for the past week. No one in the small crew seemed to know each other well except for Steve and Squeaky, the engineers; they had obviously worked together before.

And the rest of us, strangers. Great way to meet people. I'll definitely have to do this again...

Foster looked back at her screens as the *Sea Star* turned against the movement of the barge, wondering again why she'd signed up for this run; well, she knew *why,* but pride didn't seem like a good enough reason at the moment. There was more blindly dogmatic testosterone poisoning on this tug than she experienced in all her years with the navy. Everton had made it perfectly clear since they'd set out that he'd only hired her because he hadn't had time to find anyone better, and no one on board seemed to disagree with him. It was as if having boobs made her useless as a navigator to these jerks, her opinions ignored or scoffed at. God forbid she might know what she was doing...

There was another thundering crash as a huge swell slammed into the tug, jolting her out of her self-righteous reverie. All that mattered now was getting out of this alive; she could complain to someone who cared when, *if*, they managed to thwart Leiah, and currently the odds weren't looking so hot.

The *Sea Star* lurched suddenly as the barge was hit with another big one, a towering wall of seething foam that assaulted their tow with devastating force. There was a groaning shriek as the connecting cable pulled tight. The thousand-pound weight that anchored the cable had jumped; Foster knew it and prayed silently that the drag wouldn't be too much—

The *Sea Star* jerked like a dog at the end of a short leash and stopped dead, breaching herself to the furious seas. Everton grabbed for a support and Woods fumbled for his flask, uncapping it and pouring a healthy slug into his coffee.

Jesus, what is he waiting for?

"Captain, the barge is taking on water," she said.

Everton said nothing, his scruffy face set and closed.

"Captain—"

"We're not releasing the cargo, Foster. There'll be no discussion," he snapped, and popped another handful of peanuts, staring out at the barge.

Foster studied him for a moment longer, unable to believe that any man could be this suicidal or any captain this blatantly irresponsible; he hadn't *seemed* insane when she'd met him, he'd been pleasant, handsome in a weathered way, radiating authority and self-confidence.

What had happened to that man? Who was this
sexist idiot munching on nuts in the skirt of a
raging typhoon and ignoring his navigator?

Well, fine. The cable would tear loose, the
winch plate would rip out of the deck, and they'd
dump the goddamn cargo anyway; she'd already
kissed her percentage good-bye, and if he wasn't
going to listen to the truth, he could just choke
on it.

She turned back to the screens frustrated and
nervous, wishing again that she hadn't taken the
first job to còme her way when she'd hit the
South Pacific—and hoping that they all wouldn't
choke on it with him as the *Sea Star* took another
pounding at the writhing black claws of Leiah.

■ ■ ■

Steve Baker was tired and grimy and the engine
checked fine, just as it had the day they'd left
port and every damned day since. Everton had
turned out to be one of those controlling types
that rattled under pressure, saw trouble and re-
acted by making his people jump through hoops.

*He says check the engine, it's checked; like we
sat on our asses for the last week and forgot to
make sure it was working . . .*

He and Squeak had given her a thorough in-
spection on the first run they'd made with Everton a few months back; she was a standard
direct-injection diesel that ran like a dream compared to some of the jobs they'd worked. Maybe
a little high on the horses for a tug the *Sea Star*'s
size, but no problems, then or now. He stood
tiredly in the rocking engine room for another
moment and watched it hum, the tight, hot com-

partment thick with the familiar smells of grease and sweat.

Everton had seemed like an okay captain on the last trip—but there hadn't been a fuckin' *typhoon* then, either, just a straight run from the Solomons to Vanuatu with a commercial load, cash on delivery—

There was another thundering blow to the ship and Steve stumbled, widened his stance to allow for the violent movement. What were they doing up there, anyway? Everton must've told the navigator to head directly for Leiah, the way the *Star* was getting mauled.

He sighed and turned to the door, hoping that their percentages weren't currently sinking to the bottom. He and Squeaky had weathered worse in terms of the ride, but they also usually worked for a salary; he hoped that Everton had cash on hand, if and when he cut the cargo loose. Insurance companies took too long to pay out.

Steve stepped out of the engine room and latched the door behind him, glancing back once through the porthole before nodding at Squeaky. His partner was propped up in the corridor with a cup of coffee and another one of his "historical" paperbacks.

He grinned up at Steve through his dark, short beard and cocked an eyebrow, asking the question that he already knew the answer to.

"Purring like a kitten, Squeak. I'm going to bed; don't wake me unless the ship starts to sink."

Squeaky nodded and went back to his book, never one for pointless chitchat. Probably why they worked so well together; Steve generally found that those who talked too much didn't do, and he didn't have time for people who wouldn't pull their own weight. Squeaky's hands were just as dirty as his.

He hit the cramped, muggy cabin just down the hall from the engine room and flopped down on the small bunk, not even bothering to turn on the light. Squeaky was the night owl, so they switched off on shifts when the engine needed to be in tight form—

The ship lurched again and Steve barely had time to put his hand out to keep his head from smacking into the wall.

"Terrific," he groaned, and decided that someone needed to have a word with their navigator about her plotting. She was cute if a little stand-offish—but apparently she didn't know dick about tropical storms. Squeaky had talked to her, said she was ex-navy, but Steve didn't care much about her training; she'd led them into a typhoon carrying a full load, and that was beyond stupid. Unless it had been Everton—although he couldn't imagine a captain deliberately jeopardizing his own ship . . .

In any case, it wasn't his problem; he didn't get paid to worry about what went on above. Steve wrapped the thin pillow around his face, dropped one foot to the heaving floor, and was asleep in less than a minute.

■ ■ ■

Captain Robert Everton stood tensely at the window and stared out at his future across a boiling sea. The tremendous dark swells battered at them mercilessly, tossing both the *Sea Star* and her heavy cargo pull as if they were cheap plastic toys.

We'll make it, just a storm, a storm can't do this to me, won't do this to me . . .

The thoughts, the memories, rushed through his mind unbidden and he was helpless against them, as helpless as a ship on stormy seas. He'd been a deckhand at seventeen, a helmsman at twenty; the ocean waters were his home, had watched him grow from a gawky teenager into a man. They had supported him, fed him, rocked him to sleep under starry skies; he had proposed to his girl on the shining waters of the Pacific under a half-moon, honeymooned on a rented sloop off the coast of New Zealand. When he'd bought the *Star* in his early thirties he'd become a captain, and his beautiful Sarah, a captain's wife. God, they'd been so young, so full of plans! A home, a new ship, maybe a few kids when they were ready . . .

Except Sarah had been taken from him by a drunk in a pickup truck a few months after she'd named the *Sea Star,* and now there was only Captain Everton and the sea, as it had been for almost thirty years. He had worked endlessly, made piddling runs from island to island, all the time tired and alone. Scraping out an existence while he saved his money for a better day, a comfortable retirement in a warm and sunny place.

And now this. He'd made this voyage a hundred times, had eased through these waters at peak season without a whitecap in sight. He'd listened to the big boys in the lanes bitch about the terrible weather while the *Star* slid by on oceans like glass. In thirty years he'd never lost a pull, never even come close.

I'll be damned *before I let a storm do this to me; you can't do this to me!*

There was another crashing blow, and Everton watched in dull disbelief as the barge seemed to pull away from them. Even through the driving rain, he could tell that the towing winch had thrown a bolt; he could feel it after knowing the *Star* for so long, could feel every inch of her and knew every shudder of her sturdy frame.

It would hold. It had to hold, or his future was gone.

"The winch is breaking loose! It's ripping up the deck!"

Everton turned, saw the girl next to him, staring out at the barge as though she knew what she was looking at. Hiring Kelly Foster had been a mistake; the woman was thoughtless, emotional—*disrespectful.*

"I've got eyes, for Christ's sake," he snapped. "And I've seen her through worse than this, Foster, so calm down and stand your station!"

He turned away, walked towards Woods to get away from the woman more than anything else. At least the helmsman had some real experience under his belt, could handle a little rough weather without acting like a child.

"Woods, keep her down-swell," he said, and the man did as he was told. He cranked the wheel, looked out the fore window—

—and his mouth dropped open, an expression of pure terror on his bruised and sweating face.

"Green water!" Woods screamed, and Everton whipped around to see the giant swell peak, a

wall of green so deep it was black. It had to be seventy, eighty feet tall—

Everton just had time to feel shock, disbelief— and an overwhelming relief that it would all be over in seconds.

Sarah, his mind whispered, and then the tons of water crashed down over them as the *Sea Star* rammed into the seething wall.

· 2 ·

Foster heard Woods scream and gripped the hard edges of the radar console reflexively. She pushed herself down into her seat, her muscles tensed against the impact.

BOOM, and the bridge keeled violently, the hiss of water all around them. A gigantic cracking sound, a cry of terror from Woods. Captain Everton was thrown into the chart table and Woods away from the helm, cups, peanuts, charts, flying across the room.

Foster was rocked back, head snapping painfully against her neck. She heard and felt metal strain around her, beneath her feet, and there was another crash as part of the *Sea Star*'s safety railing broke behind them.

She turned, actually saw the long, heavy antenna that had torn the railing spin into the watery darkness as the bridge lights flickered.

The long-range, Jesus, it snapped.

It seemed to last forever, the terrible thrashing slide of foam all around them—and then they were through the worst, the *Star* bobbing back to the roaring surface as the storm swept them on.

Foster took a deep breath and exhaled slowly, saw that the damage was minimal, considering; the windows were intact, the lights were back on—they still had a chance.

Everton rushed to the aft window before they had even settled, his lined, scruffy face horrified and searching. Foster looked past him and saw the container barge had nearly upended in the crashing wall of water, one end thrown into the air. A stack of lumber broke free, was tossed across the pull like a bundle of twigs. The top of the canister stack had torn loose and she saw several of the containers slide away and disappear into the foaming darkness as the barge smacked down into the water.

Foster could see the desperate anguish on the captain's face and felt pity for him, in spite of the fact that it was his idiocy that had caused it. She glanced at Woods, who seemed shaken but unhurt, then back at Everton, searching for something encouraging to say; the captain stared out at the loss as though his heart was breaking.

"If you were any kind of navigator . . ." he said, trailing off as though the rest were obvious.

Foster felt her skin flush as the words sank in, all other thoughts blasted away by a throbbing redness. "No, *you* put us on this course, *Captain*! You have us a hundred miles out of any normal shipping lane, we're doing a ten-day crossing in the middle of typhoon season, so don't blame this on me!"

He stepped towards her, his own face flushed and angry. "Foster, I'm the owner of this ship and her captain, goddamn it, and I'll have your respect!"

They locked stares and Foster hated him, hated his stupid, irresponsible attempt to shift blame, to control her, to kill them all by sending them into a *typhoon*—

—and he calls the shots here, sailor, not you. Her father's voice, a cool reminder of her past and a warning for her future.

And right as always; shit.

She gritted her teeth and heard her own voice respond, defiant but tightly controlled.

"Yes, *sir*," she spat, and looked away before the hate could take hold again.

"Captain, we're taking on water," said Woods. "I can feel it, I'm losing her . . ."

Everton stalked past her to the helm, and she turned back to her screens, furious as another swell tossed them up and dropped them back into the churning waters.

Foster didn't want to die, but her reasons had narrowed suddenly to a single-minded goal, a thought to hold on to in the chaos of the storm. She wanted them to make it, wanted to feel the dock solid beneath her feet when she bid Captain Everton farewell with a right cross to his ridiculous, incompetent face. He was only captain of the *Sea Star;* off her planks, Foster could do as she damn well pleased.

■ ■ ■

Steve was jerked from an uneasy sleep to the shrill and pulsing shriek of an alarm. He was on his feet before he could think clearly and was slammed into his cabin door for his troubles. The *Sea Star* lurched again and he shook his head, remembered the storm, and found his legs.

The corridor was as tight and humid as his cabin, only much brighter, a red flash punctuating each deafening cry of the alarm. Steve rubbed at his eyes and Richie and Hiko were suddenly there, both men looking as tired and unhappy as he felt.

"It's the engine alarm! Come on!" Richie shouted, and Steve was wide-awake as soon as he heard "engine." *Damn it,* what could have happened? He couldn't have been asleep for more than a few minutes—

He turned and ran, the two deckhands behind him, and saw Squeaky's chair overturned in front of the door to the engine room at the end of the corridor. His partner was staring through the thick glass porthole set into the door, his expression tense beneath the flashing crimson light.

Squeaky stepped out of the way as Steve grabbed the latch and slapped it down—and nothing happened.

"It's buckled," said Squeaky, and Steve was already scanning the frame, still jiggling on the useless handle and pushing against the door. God, it must have been a big one to jam the thick panel into place—a flaw in the metal exploited by the furious storm.

He raised his head, looked through the hatch window—and felt ice water hit his veins and electrify every part of his exhausted body.

Green seawater gushed through a rip in the

aft bulkhead, poured into the locked room in a tiny foaming river.

Steve threw himself into the steel door once again, but it wouldn't give, didn't even rattle against the frame.

"If that water stalls the engine, we're fuckin' dead," said Richie, and Steve turned, struggled to think straight in the shuddering, screaming corridor.

He looked up into the tattooed face of the silent man behind him, organizing his thoughts even as he spoke. "Hiko, get a torch and cut the door off."

Squeaky'll take over, Richie can assist.

"I'm going above," he finished, and all three of the men nodded; they understood what they needed to do without having it spelled out. Steve silently thanked Everton for having enough sense to hire hands with brains and then he was running, headed through the flashing red hall for the ladder that would lead him to the bridge.

■ ■ ■

Everton paced the swaying floor, fists clenched, a pounding headache firmly in place from the screaming, flashing alarms. He looked back at the barge, watched another four containers wash away, lost to the swirling black waters. In spite of the loss of ballast, the pull sat low in the tossing seas, too low . . .

. . . but there's still plenty left, it's not all gone, it's not—Jesus, that alarm is driving me insane*!*

"Turn that damned noise *off*!"

Foster fumbled at a panel and the shrieking stopped, the lights flashing silently now; at least she was good for something, terrific, that was just *fine*.

Everton's gaze was drawn again to the gradually sinking barge; he couldn't watch, *couldn't,* but he couldn't look away for more than a second or two, either. It was everything, and nobody understood, nobody cared.

Foster had been tapping at her screens, trying to look busy as his life slipped away. She was an idiot, Woods was an incompetent—the engine alarm had probably gone off because Baker and his man had screwed something up—

"Captain, recommend new course heading of—two two nine degrees," Foster said. "We'll find the eye, it's only an hour and a half out . . . Captain?"

It was impossible. The only way to break the eye wall was if they cut the barge loose, and Foster knew it. What did *she* have to lose?

"We don't have an hour and a half," he murmured, and watched as another several barrels slid away, sank beneath the waves. Lost, so much of it lost now . . .

The woman would not stop. "Captain, once we're in the eye we'll have calm seas for almost two hours; we could make repairs and steady the barge."

Did she think he couldn't hear the pause, the mocking tone in her shrill voice? They didn't have the power to make it through the worst of the storm, not with the weight of the pull—

Woods spoke urgently. "Captain, I need an answer on that."

They're all against me, all of them.

Why couldn't the *Star* have just gone down, just given him some peace? What had he done to deserve this, to be forced to watch his life torn away?

There was a blast of noise from below and Everton turned, saw Steve Baker climb onto the bridge.

"What the hell's going on up here, Captain? The engine room's taking on water!"

Everton felt a surge of anger and self-righteousness; he turned on the younger man, fuming.

"Then pump it out, mister, you're the bloody engineer!"

"We can't get in! The bulkhead door took a hit and it's wedged tight, Hiko's cutting in now—"

Foster broke in. "Winds one-twenty!"

Baker ran his hands through his hair, looked around the bridge—and his gaze caught the heaving tow behind them.

"The barge! You've gotta be fucking *kidding* me." He stared at Everton, incredulous. "We've got to cut it loose."

"That's not an option, Baker," he replied. It was foolishness, cowardice—

"Captain, should I head for the eye? I need an answer, I'm losing her!" Woods asked.

"Winds one twenty-five, sir—"

"I gotta have an answer!"

The woman and the incompetent, and now Baker again, resentful, malicious.

"Captain, I'll put it real simple for you—if that barge sinks, we sink with it!"

Everton shook his head. *I am captain, I'm captain here!*

"A chance I'll take," he growled, barely able to suppress his rage at the blatant disloyalty, the willingness of them all to see him destroyed.

Baker stared at him a moment longer and then turned, headed for the stairwell that led out onto the howling deck. "I'm cutting it loose," he said, and Everton felt something inside snap.

He drew his revolver and leveled it at Baker, the weight of it in his hand good, powerful. He saw fear on the engineer's boyish face, fear and respect for the gleaming weapon.

"Move away from that door," he said, and felt his control return in a hot surge of adrenaline; *he* was captain, he would make the decisions, and no one was going to take that away from him.

Baker would stand aside or he'd find out the hard way that Everton meant what he said.

• 3 •

Foster stared at the captain in stunned disbelief as the *Sea Star* rocked wildly in the raging typhoon. She rose from her seat on numb legs but didn't leave her console, afraid to draw Everton's attention.

He hates me enough already—Jesus, he's nuts!

She could see the same disbelief on Steve's face, astonishment and a sudden angry curiosity. "What's so precious about that cargo, what the hell you got back there? Drugs? Gold bouillon? The insurance company'll eat the loss, Captain! Am I missing something here?"

Everton's faded blue eyes were wild, his voice desperate. "The cargo's *mine*, I—I leveraged everything I own and it isn't insured!"

Everything clicked into place—the anger, the blame-laying. Foster suddenly understood why he'd done this, why he'd risked the lives of

everyone on board rather than jettison the
barge. There had to be hundreds of thousands
of dollars at stake—

—and he'll see us all dead before giving it up.
The engineer saw it, too, and Foster could tell
that it wasn't going to stop him. Steve moved
again towards the door.

Everton pulled back the hammer smoothly,
cocking the long barreled .455 Webley.

Steve shook his head in exasperation. "I go
out that door, you'll shoot me; I stay here, we
all drown!"

The captain couldn't hear him, just as he
hadn't heard Foster or Woods. "I'm warning
you, mister!"

Steve glared at him for another second and
Foster held her breath, wondered if she could
make it to Everton in time; a step and a jump,
he wasn't looking at her . . .

Steve turned and grabbed for the door just as
the *Sea Star* was pitched forward suddenly,
throwing them all across the bridge.

Foster hit the console, bounded off into the
same railing that caught Everton; she heard
Woods trip and fall behind them. Steve was
tossed against the side of the stairwell and came
up fast, ready to charge the captain.

They all heard it then, the whiplike, springing
thwapp of cabled steel snapping.

Foster looked through the storming night and
saw the shredded cable give, lash across the top
deck to tear out more of the safety railing and
knock the cheap aluminum lifeboat off its
mount. The small boat was immediately torn
away by the storm—and the heavy barge disappeared behind a swell, lost from view.

Seconds ticked by and the *Star* kicked up, gave them all a clear view of the cargo barge as it slipped beneath the waves. Everton's obsession was gone.

For a moment, nobody spoke, all of them staring out at the vast and blustering sea. Foster could feel the change, imagined they all could—the *Sea Star* had more power, had lightened suddenly and smoothed in the turbulence. The waters were still rough, but without the drag of the container barge, their chances had improved about a hundred percent.

Foster looked at Captain Everton, who dropped his gaze to the revolver in his hand as if he didn't understand how it had gotten there. After a moment, he eased the hammer down and reholstered the weapon.

Steve stared at the captain, his eyes bright and flashing with anger. "Let me tell you something," he said softly, and took a menacing step towards Everton, hands tightening into fists. "If you *ever* pull a gun on me again, I'll . . ."

"You'll what?" said Everton, but the fight had gone out of him. He seemed defeated, his shoulders slumped.

Foster moved past the captain and took Steve's arm, pulled him back towards the ladder. Everton still *had* the weapon, and the tempers were too high, the storm too strong, for them to lose their engineer.

"You figure it out," said Steve, but he let Foster lead him, still glaring at Everton.

"Stand your station, Foster," said the captain, but it came out bluff and weak; she ignored him. Getting the engineer off the bridge, getting *herself* off the bridge, was more important right now. Woods had the coordinates; let him deal with Everton.

She watched Steve go down and then started after him, suddenly more tired than she could remember being in years.

■ ■ ■

Everton watched them leave, watched Foster defy him openly, and then turned to Woods. The helmsman wouldn't meet his gaze, but Everton was too angry to care.

"Woods, enter in the ship's log—oh four hundred hours, Captain Robert Everton jettisoned cargo barge to preserve the lives of *Sea Star* crew. Captain was unaware of impending typhoon conditions, owing to the failure of meteorologist and navigator Kelly Foster, *female,* to inform."

He turned back to the window, saw only simmering water where his future had been, and felt the anger die. It didn't matter anymore, none of it. They could all go to hell.

Woods cleared his throat nervously. "Captain, what about Foster's idea? We can reach the eye . . . Captain?"

Everton stared out at the ocean, the massive swells whipped into foam by the winds, torn apart and then rising again, endlessly. After a while he heard Woods make the changes that would take them to the eye, and that didn't matter, either.

. . . *gone, gone, gone* . . .

He stood there for a very long time, Captain Everton and the sea.

· 4 ·

It's comin' in faster than it's goin' out," said Squeaky, and Steve sighed and nodded. Even with the pumps on full, the level in the engine room wasn't dropping. It had been hip-deep an hour ago and now it sloshed against Steve's navel. Water shot out of the open deck hatch, the hum of the pumps' generator the only mechanical sound in the eerie quiet of Leiah's bizarre, unblinking eye.

They'd made it just before dawn, broken through the eye wall in a final, frantic push and been received by a strange and unreal calm. When the sun had come up, Steve had taken five and gone out on deck for a long look; he'd never seen anything like it.

The *Sea Star* floated gently a few miles in front of a solid bank of fog, thick and swirling. The fog extended out and around in a curve, blocking much of the eye from view; beyond was the storm itself, impossibly tall walls of dark and solid driving rain. The sea pitched mildly beneath the tug, under a ragged but distinctly circular patch of clear morning sky overhead. They were in the vacuum caused by the wildest of the gusting winds, the eye wall; Leiah raged on, but the *Sea Star* was in a soundless, pressurized pocket, only the lap of water against the hull and the soft noises of human beings at work in the still, moist air.

Steve was exhausted and frustrated and extremely goddamn cranky. Having his balls immersed in murky salt water was certainly helping to keep him awake, but did nothing for his state of mind. The engine room was flooded, the marine diesel shut down and half submerged, along with him and Squeak—and the pumps weren't enough, not anymore. The *Sea Star* had taken too much damage as she'd made her thrashing way through the storm; tiny holes in the hull had been battered into rips and tears that seeped unseen. Already she sat too low in the water.

All thanks to the good captain . . .

Foster had given Steve an earful when they'd gotten below, away from that crazy fuck; he was still fuming.

Squeaky was already gathering his scuba gear for an outside look, sloshing through the room to pick up a tank. Steve shook his head, wondering if the others had any idea how bad it really was; they were screwed, no two ways about it. If they couldn't patch it over, the ship would sink.

"How could we be so stupid to sign up with this guy again?"

Squeaky shrugged. "The fucker pulled a gun on you? I'da decked him."

Steve wished he had. "The bastard had us pullin' five hundred tons of steel and lumber, *uninsured*, a hundred miles from any normal shipping lane in a *typhoon*. Our helmsman's a weasel, our navigator's a . . ."

Squeaky grinned and muttered something in Spanish; Steve only picked up "hot" from the Cuban vernacular.

Steve scowled. "Ah, she got drummed out of the navy for striking a superior officer—"

He broke off, realizing that he'd just been thinking about doing pretty much the same thing. He looked around and shook his head again, not wanting to talk about Foster anymore.

"I can't *believe* this," he said, and hoped that Squeaky wouldn't notice the change of direction; he kind of liked Foster, or at least didn't dislike her, and Squeaky would tease him mercilessly if he knew it.

Squeaky was still smiling. "So Foster has a problem with authority; you're not the coolest cucumber either, Steve." He picked up his tank and heaved it out of the hatch as he spoke. "But I'll tell you this, this is the last time we work for percentage of the cargo instead of a salary."

Might be the last time we do anything, Steve thought, and then boosted himself up after Squeaky to find out for sure. With any luck, they could fix the problem and make it out Leiah's other side. If it was as bad as it seemed right now, though, not getting paid was going to be the very least of their troubles.

■ ■ ■

Foster stood out on the jutting wing bridge with Richie, the two of them inspecting the damage to the radio system in the heavy, strange air. The long-range antenna had been snapped off almost at the base, which was bad enough—but the coupler had also shattered into multiple pieces, and that meant rigging a replacement wasn't going to happen.

On the top deck below them, Steve was helping his partner into a dive suit and Hiko was busy with a torch, leaning against what was left of the safety railing. Woods had crashed for a short spell and Everton was nowhere in sight; she hadn't seen him in over an hour. Rays of sun pierced through the fog, made the scene look almost peaceful; a day of hard work on an ocean tug in the tropics . . .

Richie stared out past the men, his dark features intent as he studied the silently raging storm beyond. He'd made it clear that he didn't want to talk to her, ignoring her attempts to start a conversation; maybe this was an opening. In spite of her irritation with the sullen attitude of the crew, she was tired of feeling like an outsider.

"That inner wall may be as high as forty-five thousand feet," she said. "The eye, twenty to thirty miles across."

Richie seemed interested. "Weird. I've never been in the eye of a hurricane before."

"Typhoon. In the South Pacific it's called a typhoon."

Richie glanced at her, sneering slightly. "Thank you very much for that," he said, words dripping sarcasm.

Jesus, what's it gonna take?

Foster stared at him, wondering why she even bothered. He was stoned half the time anyway . . .

Richie crouched down, scooped up a chunk of the broken coupler, and sighed heavily. "This thing's history."

Foster looked out across the deck and watched as Squeaky plunged overboard, the splash loud in the unnatural quiet of the eye. Steve ran a hand through his thick, dark hair and paced back and forth a few steps, looking down into the rippling water. Tall, but not too tall. Well built, definitely, good-looking in a preppy kind of way—

She realized suddenly that she was checking him out and turned back to Richie, surprised at herself. She gave it another shot. "Couldn't you bypass that capacitor, rewire it . . . ?"

"On an antenna coupler, it's a resistor, not a capacitor. I don't talk to you about navigation, so don't talk to me about electronics, okay?" He stood up, his low words stinging and sharp.

Foster glared at him. "Could you please explain the problem you have with me? Are you mad at me *today,* or is this a female thing?"

Richie's expression remained blank, his dark eyes unreadable. "No, no, don't get me wrong, Foster. I *love* women, I just don't think they should be on a boat."

He tossed the piece of mangled equipment to the floor and started to walk away—then stopped and turned, and Foster could see the anger now, the reality behind his little speech.

"I know who your father is. We all needed the money a hell of a lot more than you did."

Foster called after him as he started walking again, unable to let it ride. "That's right, Richie,

I have a trust fund and a Park Avenue apartment, this is just a hobby! I love this, I love sleeping in a closet and using the head after Woods—"

She was talking to air; Richie had walked out, headed for the top deck where Steve and Hiko waited for Squeaky to come up with news. Frustrated, she kicked at the ruined coupler, sent it skittering across the boards.

She took a deep breath, turned and looked out at Leiah. The raging storm mirrored her feelings perfectly; she'd made mistakes, a lot of them, but it wasn't her fault that she was an admiral's daughter, or that both of her parents were successful. And it wasn't fair that Richie blamed her for it, assuming that she was some kind of debutante just because she came from money.

Her father's voice was tough, unforgiving. *You gonna give up then, sailor? Throw in the towel because some classist asshole thinks he's better than you? You have the skills, Kit, you worked hard to get them; don't let anyone tell you that you don't belong here.*

"Right again, sir," she whispered, and let the anger go in another deep breath, blown out slowly. She'd had to prove herself before, and she was at least as smart as anyone else on the tug . . .

Foster squared her shoulders and headed off to get a cup of sorely needed coffee, which she would drink out on the deck with the others. They didn't want her there? Too bad; her ass was on the same line as theirs and she wasn't going to run off crying because Richie or Everton or any of them didn't like it.

I am woman, hear me roar—or get the fuck out

of my way, she thought, and found herself smiling for the first time in much too long. Just let Everton try to ignore her now.

■ ■ ■

The captain sat at the battered desk in his quarters and stared down at the clutter, feeling old and tired and more than a little drunk. Papers and photos lay across the crowded desktop, a few words distorted and magnified by a shot glass that was somehow empty again.

My whole life, right here, he thought miserably. *Sitting on my own goddamn ship, sitting here with my whole life right in front of me . . .*

It was pathetic, the small spread of papers that made up who he was. Financial records from the bank that spanned decades, told of every hard-earned deposit and every meager withdrawal—up until the last one, of course. There was a picture of his tiny house in Guam, sold now; not even a place to hang his hat when they made it to land . . .

"Not *gonna* make it," he mumbled, and reached for the shot glass and the half-empty bottle. Whiskey, and not even a decent brand. Everton felt a drunken self-pity well up inside and hated himself for it, which only made the feelings stronger.

At least there would be no witnesses to talk about his failure, to tell people what had happened. The *Sea Star* was still taking on water; he could feel her heaviness, her slow and inevitable settling into the sea. His beautiful little tug was going to sink unless the crew managed to stop it somehow, and they weren't good enough.

The crew, *his* crew. They hated him, but did he care? Jokes, the whole lot. A bitch navigator, an ass-kissing helmsman, a couple of screwed-up deckhands—a primitive with tattoos on his face and a pot-smoking black. And the engineers— he'd expected more from them, the only two he'd worked with before, but they wouldn't be able to plug a bottle with a cork; pretty boy and his Cuban pal, probably buggered each other anyway.

He poured the cheap whiskey with shaking hands and a few drops splashed across a snap- shot of the *Sea Star,* taken on the day he'd brought her home. He brushed the liquid off and held it up, studied it. There he was, young and strong, grinning like a man without a care in the world; he was standing in front of the tug proudly and wearing the captain's hat that his young, pretty wife had bought for him. Sarah had taken the picture, and he could remember her laughing, making him don the cap for the posed shot. She'd been wearing a dress, green with tiny white flowers . . .

Gone, Sarah, everything's gone now.

Everton picked up the glass and downed it, felt the fire pour down his aching throat and loosen the knot in his belly. It would all be over soon, one way or another.

The captain poured himself another drink and carefully avoided looking at the revolver that lay across one corner of his desk; it wasn't time, not yet. He wanted to finish the bottle and look through the pictures, remembering what it had been like to still have dreams. He picked up a photo of himself at age eighteen. "I've let ya down, lad."

• 5 •

Steve watched for bubbles over the side of the *Sea Star* and felt his spirits sink lower with each passing minute; he could see the air rising to the surface, Squeak was fine—but the longer he stayed down, the more likely that it wasn't good news.

Hiko had laid aside his tools for the moment and started watching with him, his inked face solemn in the morning light. Steve had wondered about the deckhand, about his culture, but hadn't wanted to ask any intrusive questions; Hiko, like everyone else on board, kept pretty much to himself. And now certainly didn't seem to be the time for Maori Q and A, with the *Sea Star* pulling water in the eye of a typhoon.

Richie joined them, pushed himself up on the rail next to Hiko, and pulled a joint out from behind one ear. He lit up, inhaling the pungent

smoke deeply as the three of them waited for
Squeaky to surface.

Steve frowned slightly. It seemed like a monumentally stupid time to get high, but he supposed that everyone had their own way of
dealing; for him and Squeaky, it was work.
Maybe Richie worked better stoned; he'd known
a few guys who could do that . . .

Hiko looked at Richie, his broad, distinctive
features flat and expressionless beneath the
etched lines on his face. "You're a strange duck,
Richie," he said, the New Zealand accent strong
in his low voice.

Richie motioned with the lit smoke at Hiko's
face and arms. "That's saying something, coming
from a human wall of graffiti. I mean, are you
people actually under the impression that those
things are attractive? And what kind of name is
Hiko, anyway?"

Hiko grinned suddenly, probably realizing that
Richie was yanking his chain. He started to rise
menacingly, as if to tackle the toking man.

"Give it a rest," said Steve, and Hiko sat down
again, his grin fading.

"Hiko is Maori. I am Maori. The tattoos are
my spiritual armor."

Richie clenched the joint between his teeth
and rolled up one sleeve, revealing a U.S. Navy
tattoo, complete with anchor. "We do it a little
differently where I come from."

Steve was surprised. "Navy? Come on . . ."

Richie nodded, serious. "Six years with the
Seventh Fleet. Weapons technology specialist,
first class. Graduated top of my class."

Steve cocked an eyebrow. "So what happened?"

Richie took another hit and pushed off the railing, exhaling the answer as he walked away.

"Drugs."

Steve grinned as Hiko turned back to his work, cutting steel plates with an acetylene torch as patches for the hull. The Maori was right, Richie *was* a strange duck.

He studied the tattooed man, looking down at the small club tucked into Hiko's belt. It looked likc a tribal thing, and he decided that there was no time like the present; hell, he might not have another chance.

"You really a Maori warrior, Hiko? Is that why you carry that club?"

Hiko didn't even look up. "It's a *wahaika*."

"A what?"

"A *wahaika*. My grandfather gave it to me." He pulled it from his belt, holding it out so that Steve could take a closer look. It was smooth and solid-looking, with intricate artwork carved into one side. A nice piece of work.

Hiko went on, quite seriously. "It carries the name of one of my ancestors, 'Hiko.' My grandfather reckons whoever carries the name Hiko and this *wahaika* can face his greatest fear and will not die."

Stevc smiled. "Know what my greatest fear is? Women. Let one get under your skin and all of a sudden you have three kids and a twenty-year mortgage. Not me, I'm seein' the world. So what's yours?"

Hiko didn't smile. "Water," he said, and went back to cutting the thick metal without another word.

Steve swallowed heavily, reminded of where they were and what they were up against. It occurred to him that he didn't really believe they were going to sink, that he hadn't accepted it as a likely outcome in spite of the facts. Watching Hiko so intent on his work made him realize that he was being foolishly naive.

Come up with a smile, Squeaky, he pleaded silently, and went back to watching the bubbles.

■ ■ ■

One by one, all of the crew assembled out on the deck to wait for the engineer to give them the word—except for Captain Everton, but Foster wasn't particularly surprised. A little curious maybe, but not surprised.

Probably off mourning the loss of his money, she thought. What an asshole. His ship was sinking and he was off crying about lost merchandise, maybe hiding from the crew that he may have doomed to a watery grave; some captain.

She sipped at her coffee and waited quietly with the others, feeling pretty good, all things considered. Neither Richie nor Woods would look at her, but Steve had given her a friendly nod and Hiko had smiled when she'd walked out on deck.

Terrific. We may be going under, but at least I'm not a social outcast anymore.

She knew it was stupid, but it didn't affect her good mood; the *Sea Star* was in easy waters, at least for a while, and she had a strong feeling that everything was going to work out. Just being alive after the night they'd had felt like an omen; surviving a typhoon was a miracle all by itself.

There was a sudden rush of bubbles over the side of the deck and the engineer surfaced, treading water easily. He lifted his face mask up and looked at them, his expression grim behind a dripping beard.

"It's bad," he said, and Foster felt her good mood melt away at his tone of voice—there was a finality to it, cold and unconditional.

"Define bad," said Steve.

Squeaky shook his head and caught on to the deck. "We're sinking."

"That's bad," mumbled Richie. Even from five feet away, Foster could smell the heavy scent of marijuana on his breath.

Hiko turned towards her, his mild brown eyes unhappy. "How far to the nearest beach?"

"Eighteen to twenty hours to the Kermadec Islands," she said quietly.

Steve frowned. "I can squeeze an hour out of that engine, tops."

Hiko stared out at Leiah's churning wall in the distance, his low voice hollow and bleak. "We're never gonna make it."

Richie turned his stoned, red-rimmed gaze to Foster. "So what do we do now? You got a suggestion, princess?"

He didn't even sound malicious, just scared, and Foster looked at the empty mount where the lifeboat had been and shook her head slowly.

So much for women's intuition.

The long-range was down, the engine was going under, and Leiah wasn't going to sit still while they floundered. It was no longer just a possibility; unless they came up with something fast, they were going to die out here.

■ ■ ■

Hiko Alailima stared out at the storm and was afraid, but he refused to let that fear get the better of him. He sat cross-legged on the deck, alone; the *Pakeha* had gone inside, to search for a solution to the problem of death. They were afraid, too, and he hoped they would find an answer—but death would still be there, whether the sinking boat made it to land or not. Hiko knew it and wanted to be at peace with the prospect, especially now that it was so close. Besides, he was a deckhand; there wasn't anything he could do on the bridge that would make a difference.

It wasn't death that frightened him, it was *how* he died. His parents had both drowned off the north coast of Aotearoa when he was still a child, leaving him and his sister, Kukupa, to be raised by their grandparents; both of his *tipuna* had been warm and loving, instilling a strong sense of cultural pride and history in their wards, but Hiko had never forgiven the sea for taking his mother and father. And he had grown to believe that the *moana* wanted to take him, too; he'd suffered terrible nightmares as a child, of being dragged down into the silent, terrible dark, unable to breathe, the corpses of his family and friends hovering beneath the waves and beckoning to him with pale arms . . .

He held the *wahaika* in his hands, drawing strength from the smooth, heavy stone that had belonged to another Hiko, nine generations before. It was strange, that the club felt so powerful to him; he was proud to be a Maori, proud to bear the *moko* on his face and body—but he was also a grown man of the late twentieth century. A lot of people saw the Maori markings and assumed that he ran around naked and howling when the moon was full, beating on drums and performing heathen rituals to make the rain fall or the sun shine; ridiculous. Being proud of his heritage didn'f make him an idiot.

That made it all the stranger, that he was here at all. He'd worked as an arc welder with a construction company for years, helped put his little sister through college and had a comfortable apartment not far from his grandparents' *pa~*. He had been happy, or at least content.

When his grandmother had died last year of a stroke, the nightmares of his youth had returned with a vengeance; it had gotten so bad that he had started drinking heavily, just to get to sleep at night. His work had suffered, he'd lost weight—and his grandfather had suggested that he face his fears, not from Maori tradition but from a talk show he'd watched about phobias.

Hiko smiled, thinking about his family, his *whanau*. Kukupa had told him he was crazy to go out on the water; she said his night terrors would be better handled by a shrink, that the idea was so much macho bullshit. She was a smart cookie, his *tuahine,* and he'd felt like an idiot explaining his decision to her. Looking out at the eye wall of the terrible *a~wha~,* he almost wished he had taken her advice.

And yet . . .

The dreams had stopped when he'd signed up for his first run as a deckhand, nine months ago. He was still afraid of the water, but he could sleep again and he'd given up drinking; he'd made plans to return home, having faced his fear successfully. Just one last run, on a small tug that was headed for Aotearoa, to a port not far from where he'd grown up. He'd taken the job on the *Sea Star* rather than fly, a final proof of his personal victory . . .

Can't get any more final than this, can it?

Hiko watched the waters lapping at the deck, definitely higher than they had been only a few hours before, and wondered at the irony of it. And he wondered at the very strangest thing, the thing that had led him to sit here and think about fear and death and what his life had been about.

In spite of the seeming futility of the *Sea Star*'s current situation, when he held the *wahaika*, he honestly felt that he wouldn't drown—that he *couldn't*, that the spirit of his namesake watched over him and would keep him safe. The club felt right in his hands, it felt like *taonga*—more than just an heirloom, it held a spiritual power for him that he couldn't deny. Maybe it was primitive to believe in such things, but right now it was all he had.

So is it real or do I just want it to be?

He didn't know the answer to that, but he suspected he was going to find out very soon. And he was afraid, but he would put a warrior's face on because he was Maori, and strength of character was as important to him as knowing the names of his ancestors. He realized now that he had not faced his fears and won; he had only stopped the nightmares, and pretended that it was over.

The true test was almost here. Hiko stared out at the waters and wondered who the victor would be.

▪ 6 ▪

Mayday, Mayday, Mayday. This is MV *Sea Star* Uniform Foxtrot Juliet India, latitude twenty-nine degrees forty minutes south, longitude one seventy-nine degrees fifteen minutes east. Taking on water in heavy seas . . ."

Foster clicked to receive, and Steve held his breath, hoping desperately to hear something, *anything*—but there was only static, the same as for the last half hour. The two of them were alone on the bridge, but neither spoke, still searching for a human voice in the haze of crackling radio silence.

He closed his eyes, amazed at man's deep capacity for optimism in the face of disaster. With the long-range down, they had a snowball's chance that anyone would hear them—and yet he still half expected to hear a response each time Foster pushed that button, still felt his gut knot in disappointment with every fruitless attempt.

Optimism or stupidity, maybe. Either way, he needed to get some air or he was going to start breaking shit, he was that agitated. She started again, her voice low and clear in spite of the strain that he saw in her face and in her tight shoulders.

"Mayday, Mayday, this is MV *Sea Star* ..."

Steve walked out onto the raised wing bridge to stand with Squeak and Richie, the two men staring out at Leiah through the thickening fog. Woods would be up in a minute to give Foster a break; Steve had seen the helmsman in the galley, stocking up on liquor. Everton still hadn't bothered to show his face, which was fine with Steve; he didn't want to waste one minute of whatever time they had left breathing the same air as that nut-ball.

Squeaky looked away from the distant storm and nodded tensely as Steve joined them. "She gettin' anything on the radio?"

Steve shook his head. "VHF only has a fifty-mile range. Better break out the survival gear."

Richie looked fuzzy, out of it. "Where the hell's the captain?"

It was a rhetorical question, and neither Steve nor Squeaky bothered answering. They stood silently, watching the storm, and Steve wondered how much time they had left.

They hadn't actually discussed the options as a crew, probably because they all knew what would happen. Steve figured they could afford to keep hailing for maybe another half hour or so, then they'd have to move the *Sea Star* before the engine went under. They'd head for the eye wall opposite to the storm's direction, put on the jackets, and wait, maybe an hour or two, bailing until water hit the bridge. When she went under, they'd bob helplessly along until Leiah swept over them, separated them—

—and then we die; the end to a perfect day.

He'd been thinking about the obvious alternative he supposed they all had; faced with the particularly nasty thrill ride that Leiah offered, you'd have to be crazy not to consider it—opting out early, taking a deep breath before the storm hit and then taking off your life jacket. Not a nice thought, but maybe better than the prospect of being battered to death by raging waters, drowned by rain, or forced under to drown anyway.

Steve didn't think he could do it. It wasn't that he relished the idea of the struggle, he just didn't think he had it in him to give up, no matter how much the odds were against his survival. He'd always believed that while there was still life, there was hope—and the thought of letting himself slip beneath the waves, to die without a fight . . . he couldn't imagine it. As far-fetched as it was, there was always that one-in-a-million chance that the storm could blow out, another ship could happen along—hell, the hand of God could reach down and pull them all to safety, for that matter. He wouldn't take off his life jacket for the same reason he'd never seriously considered suicide, even in the worst of times; things could always change. He glanced over his shoulder, saw Woods and Hiko walk onto the bridge. Foster let Woods take her seat, moving over to the navigator's console. She had a nice body, well endowed but athletic, tight; a strong, intel-

ligent face. Great eyes. He thought about what
he'd said to Hiko earlier about women, and wondered why he didn't feel that way when he
looked at Foster . . .

He shook his head; it didn't matter now, did
it? Richie and Squeak were heading in to join
the others, and Steve followed, still hoping somehow that their call for help would be answered
and still struggling to accept that it was highly
fuckin' unlikely.

■ ■ ■

Foster stared down at the radar screen blankly,
listening to Woods's growing frustration with the
VHF radio. The bridge was tense, the crew
standing around silently, mulling over their pre-
dicament while the helmsman SOS'd into dead
air. She wondered if anyone had told Everton
about the situation, not that it would make a difference. At least she wasn't alone in her dislike
for the man anymore; everyone in the room
knew what had happened . . .

The radar still worked, for what it was worth.
All the receiver had to say was that they were
surrounded by a typhoon, at least in the range
that the CW was set for. Foster tapped at the
keys in front of her, widening the scope; she
hadn't thoroughly checked out the eye for a few
hours; maybe there was something new to see.

"Mayday, Mayday, Mayday—fucking VHF
fifty-mile-range piece of *shit*—"

Blip. Foster felt her heart stop, then speed up
violently. It wasn't her imagination, it was a solid
return. "Wait a minute! I'm picking up a contact,
could be a ship in the eye with us . . ."

She could feel the change, feel everyone's sudden attention turn to her as she double-clicked the cursor on the pulse-generated object and read the coordinates.

"Distance twelve miles bearing zero four eight degrees. Speed—zero knots, appears to be dead in the water. And it's big."

She looked up, studied the intent and hopeful faces of the men on the bridge, and felt like laughing. "Really big," she said.

"Hail 'em," said Steve, and she grabbed the mike, flooded with a relief so great that she could hardly breathe. She saw Woods cast a guilty look around the bridge and then walk out quickly, probably to tell Everton. Fuck him, she was too excited to care.

"Ahoy vessel at latitude twenty-nine degrees forty-eight minutes south, longitude one seven nine degrees twenty-four minutes east, this is *Sea Star;* we are twelve miles northwest of your position, come back!"

They weren't going to die. The tug might sink, but they now had somewhere to go.

■ ■ ■

The whiskey was gone; it was time.

Sarah smiled up at him from atop the pile of papers, just as perfect and beautiful as he remembered. He hoped that she'd be there, waiting for him in whatever came next. Or maybe he'd just be dead; either way, he'd be free from having to face a dismal future, any chance of peace he could have had lost to him now.

Everton slowly picked up the loaded .45 caliber revolver and pointed it to the right of his forehead, afraid but ready. He could feel trickles of sweat slide through his hair, gray hair on his old, tired head. Old and tired and drunk, that was Captain Robert Everton. He didn't think there would be time to feel pain; just a burst of sound and he could escape from this cruel and merciless life . . .

He closed his eyes and there was a knock on his door.

"Captain. Captain!"

Woods. *Christ, what timing!*

"I'm busy," he said, and waited for the helmsman to leave, the cool barrel still pressed to his skin. Insult to injury. Even this last privacy was denied to him, a parting shot from Whomever ran this show.

"There's a ship with us in the eye! Twelve miles out, dead in the water!"

Big fucking deal, some other poor bastard caught in the storm, like I'm gonna give a rat's ass when my life is—

Dead in the water. Everton blinked.

A ship that wasn't moving. Perhaps because the crew had bailed out or been taken by the typhoon, leaving their vessel behind . . .

Everton lowered the weapon and tried to focus his bleary thoughts on what this meant, what it *could* mean.

Salvage, reward money, navigational equipment. Expensive equipment. A ship . . .

"Dead in the water? I—I'll be there in a moment," he said, and he heard his helmsman's footsteps scurry away.

He stood up too quickly, felt the cabin wobble and then reestablish itself. He holstered the sidearm and wiped the back of his hand across his forehead, then hastily pushed the stack of papers and photos into a desk drawer.

He ducked into his private head and splashed water across his face and into his mouth, blotting his skin with a hand towel. The polished steel mirror reflected back a presentable visage—tired-looking, ragged around the edges maybe, but it would do.

Everton didn't even bother locking the door behind him, too eager to get to the bridge. He heard and felt the engine fire, a low hum beneath the sagging deck of his ship as the crew prepared it to move; it was a sound he had almost given up, that he'd been seconds from giving up forever, and now he knew that it hadn't all been for no reason. It was like—a test, a crucible that he had almost failed. He felt himself sobering with each step, felt his shoulders fall back and his vision clear as he walked through the tight corridor and out onto the top deck.

A second chance, it's a sign, another moment and it all would've been over—it has to mean that it's not *over for me. I can feel it.*

He strode towards the bridge, feeling strong and reasonably steady by the time he reached the door, propped open in the thick humidity of the typhoon's eye. The entire crew was assembled, and he decided that it would be best to reassume command as though nothing had happened. Yes, that was best; he had made a mistake or two, he was only human, they'd understand. Hard feelings would be overlooked, they were all adults, grown men—well, and Foster, but one female voice wouldn't influence opinion, especially when she'd proved herself to be such a poor navigator. They'd probably be thankful to have a leader again, someone to take control.

"Woods, what the hell are you doin'? Let's *go*." Baker was trying to give orders, and Everton stepped onto the bridge to relieve the man of the burden. The engineer had a temper, but he'd have cooled off by now; everything had changed.

"Why isn't this thing moving, Woods?" he asked smoothly.

He could feel the weight of their stares, all of them, but he remained focused on the helm, exuding a calm confidence in his position as captain. They didn't have to love him to respect his orders; his earlier lapse of reason could be explained, when they were out of danger. He just had to be rational and firm, give them cause to look up to him again.

Captain Everton nodded to Woods, and the helmsman grinned and nodded back.

"Fuckin' A, Captain," he said, and turned the wheel, steering them towards salvation. The waterlogged *Sea Star* started to move, picking up speed easily as they made their way through the fog.

Everton walked to the wing bridge, already imagining the possibilities; even a tug the size of the *Sea Star* could make up for a lot . . .

A dead ship, no crew to lay claim—it was the answer to everything.

· 7 ·

The *Sea Star* chugged heavily along into the thick fog; white-gray clouds of solid mist enveloped the boat as they moved through the eye, curling lithe fingers around the hull, beckoning them deeper. Richie breathed it in, imagining that he could smell the bottom of the sea in the white air. It was a dark and musky, salty odor, like the typhoon had opened the womb of the ocean, forced her to expel secrets from deep inside. It was ... really interesting.

Richie felt good. He'd been pretty high all morning, and already the whole sinking thing was fading behind him like a bad dream; he'd been able to keep himself kind of Zen, living in the moment—the sun, the water, all that happy-crappy. Still, it had been unnerving, and he was glad to be able to kick back for a while, enjoy things without *that* nasty business looming in front of him. The admiral's brat had finally done her goddamn job, the captain was back (though he stank like he'd just crawled out of a distillery, no shit), and they were gonna be riding home in style.

He stood at the bow with Hiko and the engineer boys, all of them peering out into the dense fog; Woods and that rich bitch were up on the bridge and the captain was standing on the flying wing, back in the saddle like some whacked-out Ahab; every ship needed a captain, even shit-faced. Besides, who was he to talk? They were gonna survive, that was the thing. All was well and cool with Mrs. Thomas's boy Richard.

He stood in between Hiko and Squeaky, Steve off to the side. The young engineer caught his gaze and jerked his head towards the Maori.

Oh, right! Steve had been talking about all that tribal shit earlier and Richie had volunteered to ask about the name; the engineer seemed concerned that he'd offend the guy.

With tatts like that, how could he possibly get offended? Must be bothered all the time, tourists and all . . .

"So, Hiko. Baker says all Maori names mean somethin'. That true?"

Hiko stared into the fog. "Yeah."

Steve jumped in. "Sooo . . . what does it mean?"

The tall deckhand shrugged, started to say something, and then Foster yelled out from the bridge.

"Dead ahead, three hundred yards!"

"Woods, hail it!" Everton called back.

Voices carried well in the eye, something to do with the pressure change. Richie's ears had been popping all day. He could hear Woods easily from the bow, their resident bootlicker; guy was an ingratiating little suck-up, always reminded Richie of one of those kids that all the other kids avoided on the playground—

—like *"Hey, wait up, guys! Don't ditch me!"* Richie grinned to himself. That was Woods, all right.

"Unidentified vessel, this is the *Sea Star* approaching you from the northwest, three hundred yards out. Come back."

They all strained to hear a response; nothing. Everton suddenly screamed down to the four of them like they were a mile away and deaf.

"Dead ahead, three hundred yards!"

No shit, *el capitán; damn*. The man was soused, straight up; probably seeing double, too.

"I don't see anything," Hiko said quietly.

The fog was solid, all right, but there was a sloshing off to their left, water against something . . .

A half-sunken lifeboat drifted by, barely visible even a few feet off the deck. It was upside down, floating like a dead man in the shrouded waters.

"That ain't ours," Hiko whispered. He sounded nervous, and suddenly Richie felt his high disappear into something less mellow. Something like fear, and he was caught off guard by how hard the emotion hit him.

He could *feel* the ship, hidden just in front of their searching gazes like an unseen ghost. There was a soft creaking that made Richie's stomach knot, a forlorn and desolate sound in the silence of the eye. Something big, really big, a dead ship cloaked by the jealous mist, a monster waiting to spring . . .

Paranoid much? Chill on that shit, jumpin' at shadows like some puss—

Richie wanted to laugh at himself, but he suddenly felt like one of those dudes from a horror flick; he had a very bad feeling about this. And for just the barest fraction of a second, even though it would've meant certain death for all of them, he wished with all his heart that Foster's screens had stayed blank.

■ ■ ■

Steve watched it appear slowly, a gradual thickening of the heavy fog into a light gray wall that loomed over them. The *Star* inched closer and suddenly they could all see it: the heavy white hull of a mammoth ship, towering and ghostly in the still air.

Jesus, look at that!

The tug veered slightly and they headed along her starboard side, the *Star* dwarfed by the ship—it stretched on seemingly forever, hundreds of feet long, the full length of it lost to the creeping mist. Woods pulled back a little and the perspective widened, giving them all a clearer feel for the sheer immensity of the silent monster.

It was hard to study the ship objectively, the fog separating and re-forming between the two vessels in a way that gave only murky flashes of the top deck. It was easily the size of a passenger liner, but outfitted for a purpose that Steve couldn't figure; he could make out what looked like a giant reception dish, one, two of them, each as big as the bridge on the *Sea Star*. Bigger.

He saw a massive crane, the damaged rigging swaying and creaking in the heavy air. There were support towers for several antennas and other devices of various sizes, pipes and beams hanging awkwardly in disrepair; he recognized a few of them, but the designs were strange, some of the mechanisms completely unfamiliar. In fact, the multileveled deck was covered with equipment he didn't know. It was military, had to be—but he didn't see armaments of any kind; it didn't make sense.

She had obviously been through the storm, the water damage unmistakable—but there was also a dark residue on parts of the deck that looked like ash, wide patches of the uniform white paint blackened by fire or electrical burns.

—but it's superficial, all of it. Why aren't they answering? Where are they? Even a typhoon wouldn't be much of a threat unless they lost their rudder; she's gotta weigh upwards of forty thousand tons.

The *Sea Star* crept along, the crew silent and uneasy as they studied the lifeless ship. Foster had walked out onto the foredeck and stood with them, as had the captain, sporting binoculars and a bullhorn. There wasn't a single light blinking, no sound except for the creak of loose riggings, no sign that anyone was aboard. The effect was dramatic and overwhelming, a gigantic vessel alone, deserted and dead.

"The lifeboats are gone," Richie said quietly, almost whispering. He sounded as freaked out as Steve felt. "All of them."

The *Star* edged up to the stern of the ship and Steve squinted at the lettering across the white hull, red and illegible. Foreign, it looked . . .

"It looks Russian," Foster said, and started flipping through the book she carried. Steve saw it was a copy of Jane's, and was glad that at least one of them had thought to bring the thick manual of listings out.

Foster stopped on a page, looked at the red lettering again and then back down. "The 'Akademic *Vladislav Volkov,* Missile and Satellite Tracking Ship.' Forty-five thousand tons full gross. Length, six hundred forty-two feet. Propulsion, two steam turbines, nineteen thousand horsepower. Seventeen knots top speed, fuel capacity not known—ship's complement, three hundred. Armament, none . . ."

Steve watched as their helmsman deftly maneuvered the *Star* around the ship's bow, still awestruck by the size and unnerved by the deathly quiet. Foster continued, reading quickly, her voice low.

"She's fitted for scientific purposes. Their biggest. Forty-two labs, five machine shops outfitted with advanced robotics . . . The three dishes can maintain simultaneous communication with several spacecrafts."

Everton raised the bullhorn and shouted suddenly, making them all jump. "Ahoy, *Vladislav Volkov*! This is the captain of the *Sea Star*! Anyone aboard? Ahoy!"

They all waited, Steve stifling his anger for Everton; the man reeked of whiskey and hadn't even bothered to apologize for being an asshole—not that Steve would've forgiven him. At least he had acted like an actual captain since he'd emerged from his private party, although Steve was going to watch his every move until they got out of this; Everton was unstable, he couldn't be trusted.

There was no answer from the *Volkov,* nothing but the hollow creak of shifting equipment. As the *Star* came along her port side, they could all see a lifeboat hanging from the davit, half submerged. There was a hole in the bottom. Steve saw the third satellite dish; the giant unit had crashed to the empty deck.

Everton turned to him, grim and authoritative. "Baker, break out flashlights and walkies . . . and bring a shotgun."

Steve hesitated, then nodded. At least the captain was thinking; they were about to board an apparently unmanned Russian vessel, and there could only be a couple of reasons for her abandonment.

Insanity. Mutiny. Mass murder . . .

He didn't like it, but there was no other choice. He took a last look at the forsaken *Volkov* and then went to get what they'd need, hoping that the ship was truly as deserted as she looked. And he was going to break out every weapon they had, just in case.

■ ■ ■

Foster stared up at the Russian ship as the *Sea Star* slowly approached, trying not to think about the *Mary Celeste.* It had been her favorite story as a child, endlessly fascinating; she must have heard it a hundred times, lingering over each mysterious detail. Now, though, she wished she could forget it; she was anxious enough, watching the port hull of the deserted *Volkov* slide closer in the softly lapping water. She should be

happy, elated; they'd found a way out of the
mess Everton had gotten them into . . .

*. . . but what happened to the crew? What
could have induced three hundred people to
abandon a ship that wasn't sinking?*

In November of 1872, the brigantine *Mary Celeste* had set sail from New York to Genoa,
carrying nearly two thousand barrels of alcohol
and manned by a crew of eight. In addition were
Captain Briggs, his wife, and their young daughter. Five weeks later, the ship was found about
six hundred miles west of Gibraltar, the cargo
intact, the hull undamaged—and no one aboard.
Story had it that the tables were set for dinner,
a child's toys were found on the captain's bed,
and all of Briggs's personal effects were still in
place. There was no evidence of violence, no apparent reason for abandonment; they were just—
gone.

*And this ship, is that what happened here? Or
are we going to find bodies stacked in the hold,
the mad killer still aboard, hiding somewhere in
the dark . . . ?*

Foster folded her arms tightly, feeling chilled
and apprehensive. She and the rest of the crew
had assembled on the starboard deck of the now
distinctly sinking tug, all except for Woods; he
and Hiko would stay behind while the rest of
them boarded the *Volkov* and investigated.

Looking up at the lifeless vessel, Foster wished
she could pass on the opportunity herself, but
they'd need her to check out the navigational
equipment. The ominous enigma of the *Celeste*
had been exciting to her as a child, but she was
an adult now; things like this just didn't happen,
shouldn't happen.

Steve had been passing out weapons and small bags of equipment and had stopped in front of her. She took a pack, nodding, and then he held out a somewhat battered-looking .32 caliber Colt semiautomatic, meeting her gaze with an expression she couldn't quite read. He looked nervous but steady, and she relaxed a little. She wasn't alone in her unease, at least. And it wasn't like there were any other options open to them; the *Star* wouldn't last much longer.

Foster reluctantly took the offered weapon, checked it, and put it in her coat pocket. She knew how to handle guns but had never liked them much—particularly not when she might have to use one.

Richie stood behind her, a shotgun gripped loosely in one gesturing hand. "I don't care what Jane says, I *studied* ships like this. This is a fuckin' spy ship, man. They're not gonna like us comin' aboard."

Foster reached out and grasped the barrel of his firearm lightly, pushing it away from herself and the others. For someone who was supposed to know weapons, the man acted like an idiot.

Or someone on drugs . . .

"Do you mind?" Foster asked pointedly.

Richie glared at her but slung the weapon over his shoulder.

"Ahoy, *Volkov*! Anyone aboard?" Everton bellowed again, but didn't bother waiting for a response. He turned to Steve as the *Sea Star* came to a stop only a few feet from the huge wall of the ship's port side.

"Throw up a line," Everton said, and Steve picked up a grappling hook from the deck, the heavy rope uncoiling.

Foster and the others stepped back as Steve swung the hook and threw, the clawed metal flying up and clanking loudly against the lowest railing above. He gave it a jerk and the line tightened, the hook catching against steel pipe. First try, and Foster found herself wishing that he'd missed—that they could stay on the *Star* a bit longer, watch the Russian vessel from a safe distance . . .

Foster looked away into the fog, noticing the gradual change in the light; they had maybe another hour before Leiah hit. An hour to find out what had happened aboard their only refuge, what had occurred to leave it deserted and powerless.

Foster swallowed dryly as the two engineers shouldered their equipment and prepared to board the lifeless ship.

· 8 ·

Squeaky Molleno didn't like this shit at *all,* but there was no way he was gonna let his partner go up alone; if there was some Ruskie wacko with an ax waiting on the deck of the *Volkov,* Steve would need some coverage. Still and all, he hadn't been so nervous since he'd lost his virginity to Maria Vasquez in the back of Pop's Ford sedan in high school—and that had been a good kind of nervous; this was just fuckin' creepy. Fog all around and a sinking tug and now *this* floating horror show looming over them . . .

. . . *desgracia sobre desgracia,* one goddamn thing after another.

"You know, this is foreign soil," said Richie casually. "We're trespassing, we need the captain's permission to board her; they can legally shoot us. Just wanted everyone to know that . . ."

Terrific. Ganja boy had all the facts; a little

encouragement was *just* what they needed.

Steve started up, hand over hand, dwarfed by the giant hull of the Russian ship. Squeaky let him get a few feet and then followed, gritting his teeth in exertion as he stepped off the tug and pulled himself into the air.

The blank white of the hull seemed to go on forever, extended at least thirty feet up from the lapping water, and that was just to the lowest of the multiple railings. Squeaky concentrated on keeping balanced, on not looking anywhere except at his hands and occasionally getting a nice, clear view of Steve's butt and legs directly overhead as they scaled the sloping wall.

He heard Steve hit the deck and then his partner's strong, sweaty hand was extended down to help him aboard. Squeaky took it gratefully; he wasn't the athlete he'd been a few years ago and he felt the strain in his arms and back as he climbed through the railing, panting.

Steve took the bundled rope ladder out of the utility bag and looped it to the railing, breathing easily in spite of their climb. Squeaky scowled to himself; he'd have to get back into his daily push-ups, no shit ... Now wasn't the time to think about it, though. His heart was thumping from more than just the trek up; this sucked.

"Boarding a ship without permission? Stupid, very stupid," he said quietly. "We're gonna get *shot*."

Steve didn't answer, but Squeaky could see that he agreed on the "stupid" part. Steve was easy to read, at least for him; they'd worked together a long time, and Squeaky could tell when his buddy wasn't happy. It wasn't like there was any alternative, but still, Squeaky didn't particularly care for the idea of their deaths being legal, and he didn't like this ship. He'd boarded derelicts before and he'd never felt so totally freaked; it felt ... *haunted.*

The rope ladder secured and dropped, Steve unshouldered the shotgun and walked to the forward ladder well. They couldn't see much from where they'd boarded, the top deck well above eye level. Squeaky followed close, searching for movement and still trying to catch his breath.

They came out next to the bridge, a raised structure as big as the *Sea Star* in its entirety. Squeaky wasn't too good on distances, but the deck that stretched out in front of them looked the length of a couple of football fields. Underneath one of the huge dishes was a glass-encased control room, twenty feet above the silent deck; he saw stairwells and closed hatches, torn canvas, ladders—but no sign of life anywhere.

"Ahoy the bridge—anyone aboard!" Steve shouted, and then fell silent as they both took in the scene. From the *Sea Star,* Squeaky had only been able to make out that there was some damage through the heavy mist. The fog was just on the water, though, it hadn't reached this far up; as he stood here now, taking in the huge deck that lay exposed before them and the bridge itself, his nervousness turned to cold fear.

He saw chipped paint and punctured metal amidst coils of rope and hanging chain; he didn't recognize a lot of the support structures, little towers of pipe and sheet steel that littered the deck, but he knew the aftermath of a firefight when he saw it. The outer walls of the bridge were riddled with bullet holes, several of the windows shattered. Dim sunlight sparkled against the jagged glass, pieces of it lying on the deck outside the bridge—

—*which means that some of the shots were fired from inside; which means . . . What* does *that mean?*

That this was some really scary shit, that's what it meant. He and Steve exchanged a look, then waited silently in the mute shadows of the bridge for the others to catch up.

■ ■ ■

Everton led the others around the outside of the bridge, feeling his excitement grow with each step across the deck of the abandoned *Volkov.* This was better than he could possibly have imagined; whatever had happened here was over, he knew the feel of a deserted ship—and that meant there was nothing to stand in his way.

He crouched down beneath the starboard windows of the wing, and the others did the same behind him as they neared the door to the bridge. He was captain, it was right that he should put himself in front—and it would make his nervous crew respect him all the more.

Besides, this beauty is dead, nothing here but shadows and dust—and a little bravado will go a long way towards smoothing things over when we get to negotiations . . .

The heavy door to the bridge was slightly ajar and Everton scooted closer, gripping the shotgun tightly. In spite of his certainty that no one was aboard, he didn't want to seem careless in front of his men.

Everton rested the barrel low against the steel door and pushed it back slowly, a soft scrape of

metal against metal in the silent air. The door
opened easily—

—and a half dozen pale shapes burst out of
the darkness, frantic, inhuman, fluttering wildly.
Everton reeled back, terrified, heard the others
gasp and shout—

—and they all watched as the attackers took
to the air, a few white feathers gliding down to
rest on the deck. Terns. Fucking *birds*.

He forced himself to smile, cursing himself for
a fool as his heart eased back into some semblance of normality; he stood up and peered inside before cautiously proceeding into the
shadowy room, ready to blow away anything else
that moved.

Dull light filtered in through the windows,
barely illuminating the panels of equipment and
outlining the blocky shapes of consoles and
chairs; Everton felt himself relax. It was empty
of life, human or otherwise.

Baker stepped in behind him and squinted at
the panel of light switches next to the entry. He
clicked several of them back and forth, but nothing happened.

"Power's out," he said softly, and dropped his
bag to the floor. He pulled out a flashlight and
aimed the mote-filled beam around the spacious
bridge as the others filed in behind him.

The light showed damage wherever it fell, exposing the dark corners of the silent room in terrible detail. There were bullet holes in the walls,
and Everton saw that whole panels of instru-
mentation equipment had been smashed. There
were spatters and smears of dried blood across
the devastated consoles, bits of circuitry and
glass strewn everywhere.

"What the fuck happened here?" Steve whispered, and Everton shook his head, studying the wrecked machinery and wondering how much could be repaired.

What a waste, so much gone . . .

There was a crackle of static in the stillness and Woods's jerky, nervous voice entered the silent room.

"Captain? You see anything, Captain?"

Everton sighed and unclipped the radio unit from his belt. "You'll be the first to know, Woods," he said, and paused—it sounded like the Maori was talking from farther away, the deep voice of the deckhand mumbling something . . .

"*. . . e aku tipuna—*" The rest of the chant was lost as Woods stopped transmitting, but Everton had to stifle a grin as he tucked the walkie-talkie back into place. He'd spent some time in New Zealand, knew a few words. Hiko was *praying*.

Better pray that the Russians want this hulk back as much as I think they will, he thought mildly, and reached into his pocket for a handful of nuts.

Even damaged, the *Volkov* was worth millions. The cargo barge was nothing compared to what he was going to make off this.

■ ■ ■

Foster walked carefully around the bridge, deeply uneasy as she studied the ruined equipment. The depth of violence implied was unnerving, and she wondered what could have gone down to inspire such brutality. It was obvious from the dried brown stains that people had been hurt or killed here . . .

She looked up from a shattered computer screen and saw Squeaky looking at her, one eyebrow raised.

"Pirates?" she asked.

"Mutiny—" he said, and then Everton cut them both off.

"Pipe down. Foster, check the radio."

She already had. "It's smashed."

Steve held up a logbook, frowning. "The logs are useless unless anyone here reads Russian."

Foster glanced out the starboard windows and saw that the light was still fading, blocked by storm clouds on the horizon. "Captain, we've got less than an hour . . . Captain?"

She turned, saw Everton pacing the back wall, deep in thought.

"He's thinking, Foster," said Richie, sneering. "Something *you* were hired for."

Foster sneered back, but Richie had already turned to Everton. "Are you thinking what I *think* you're thinking, Captain?"

Squeaky frowned. "Thinkin' what?"

"Salvage," answered Steve, and Everton stopped suddenly and addressed them as a group, his eyes glittering in the murky light.

"You all signed on for a percentage, but you never figured I'd bring you this, did you? A ship abandoned in international waters. Maritime law says she's a derelict; all *we* have to do is tow her to safety, slap a salvage lien on her, and the Russian government's gotta pay us ten percent of her value to get her back. Richie, put a number on this."

Richie grinned. "Let's see . . . three parabolic satellite dishes, one's kind of fucked up—forty labs, all primed with state-o'-the-art stuff—we're talkin' . . . two, three hundred million."

Everton didn't even bother trying to contain his excitement. "Three hundred million dollars. Ten percent of that's thirty million, and that's what's coming our way. The opportunity of a lifetime—if we play our cards right."

Squeaky was frowning. "One percent of thirty million is . . . uh, what, thirty grand?"

"Three *hundred* grand, Squeak," said Steve.

"I'm willing to change that," Everton said easily, "cut all of you in for ten percent. A cool three million each. What do you think?"

In spite of her disgust for the man, her amazement at the calculated greed in his voice, just the sound of "three million" gave Foster pause; that was nothing to laugh at. She looked around, watched as the others digested the information.

Squeaky looked at Steve. "Is it legal?"

Steve nodded. "Totally."

"Then I'm in," Squeaky said, and then looked at his partner uncertainly. "Steve?"

The engineer paused for a beat and then turned to Everton, his expression blank. "Yeah. Sure, we're in."

Richie's answer was obvious, and Foster suddenly realized that they were all looking at her. She didn't say anything, not sure how she felt about the sudden turn of events; the crew was probably dead, but no one seemed to care. Whatever had happened had obviously been over for a while, but it was a big ship, lots of places to hide—they could be in danger. And Everton had glossed right over all of it, acting like he was somehow responsible for this great fortune . . .

Richie rolled his eyes dramatically. "Oh, come *on*—"

Squeaky's bright gaze was encouraging. "Go for it, easy money."

"There is no such thing as easy money," she said carefully, but she already knew that she wasn't going to turn it down. It wasn't like they were going anywhere on the *Sea Star;* and three *million*—

Everton nodded briskly at her. "I'll take that as a yes. Baker, find the ship generators, we'll need power to the bridge. See if you can get the main engines running. Squeaky, go with him."

Steve was already rummaging through his bag, producing flashlights and additional walkie-talkies to hand out. He strapped an ammo belt around his shoulder as Everton continued.

"Richie, throw a line to the tug, have her turn the ship in to the wind. Foster, see if you can get some of this navigational equipment working."

Steve and Squeaky started out the door, Richie right behind them, and Foster hesitated, watching Everton. He fairly bristled with excitement; she could almost see the dollar signs in his pale blue eyes.

"Captain, my father was an admiral and I know something about salvage law—if there's anyone alive on this ship, we can't take custody of her."

Everton barely glanced at her, fumbling for his walkie-talkie. "Then let's not find anyone alive."

She stared at him, not sure what she'd just heard. "What does *that* mean?"

Everton turned and met her gaze evenly. "Just that I hope we don't find anyone alive."

He clicked the unit and turned away, dismissing her. "Woods, come back . . ."

Foster watched him for another moment, then walked through the debris of the shattered bridge to the radar console, wondering what they had gotten themselves into—and whether their captain realized the implications of what he'd just said.

• 9 •

Steve and Squeaky moved through the still darkness of the *Volkov*'s A deck with only their flashlights to guide the way; the twin beams darted ahead of them down the long corridor, showing them an empty, sterile white hall and the occasional sign lettered in Russian. Nothing moved and there was no sound except for their own footsteps, echoing hollowly in the cool, still air.

Steve was worried; whoever had trashed the bridge had been almost methodically thorough in their attack; he didn't much like the idea of running into such a person, down here in the dark. In fact, he'd go so far as to say that he was scared shitless at the prospect; the ship *seemed* empty, but what if they were wrong?

The corridor ahead turned sharply to the left, and they edged up to it cautiously, Steve's finger under the trigger guard of the twelve-gauge. There was still no sound, no sense that anything was moving, and they went ahead.

Their lights quickly strafed the short hall and both of them stopped, staring at the door at the end. The thick metal hatch had been bent off its hinges.

"Jesus!" Squeaky whispered.

They moved through the entry, Steve trying not to think about what it would take to bend steel like that.

"Stay close, Squeak."

Doesn't matter, it already happened, whatever it was—heat, maybe somebody was welding— maybe the typhoon . . .

He shook his head, putting the ridiculous thoughts out of his mind. He wasn't thinking straight; it had been too long since he'd gotten more than a few hours' sleep. Besides, knowing what had happened wouldn't change anything; they had to get to the engine and get the power back on, first things first.

There was an open door ahead on their right and they edged up to it, shone their lights across some kind of lab room, long tables and machines lining the walls. It was as messed up as the bridge had been. Thick cables had been sliced through, equipment had been smashed, and there were pieces of paneling and wires all over the floor. Steve noticed a faint, acrid tinge to the air, like burned circuitry.

Squeaky played the beam across the heavy cables. "These were cut with an ax," he said quietly. "This is creepy, man. I'm not likin' this at all."

They moved on, and the next yawning dark-

ness they came to was the one they'd been looking for; above the Russian scribble was a stick
figure walking down stairs, the hatch open.

The beams of light danced across red smears
and spatters on the slanted walls that led down
into the dark.

"Please, God, don't let us find any bodies,"
said Squeaky, and as they started down the stairwell, Steve wondered about that.

Where are *the bodies? And if the whole crew
was slaughtered, who took the lifeboats?*

None of it made sense. They reached the bottom of the first flight and started down the next,
Steve finally giving voice to his unease as they
moved through the quiet blackness.

"I've got a bad feeling about this; it just
doesn't add up, Russian vessel sittin' out here,
no crew . . . Why would they abandon ship?"

He paused, then decided to ask outright.
"Squeak, who do you think we can trust?"

Squeaky had obviously already given it some
thought. "Forget the captain. Woods is wound
so tight you couldn't pull a pin outta his ass with
a tractor. Richie looks like a waste case, but I
gotta admit—he's sharp, man, like a fox. He'll
be there if we need him. Hiko, I can't tell yet.
Foster's good."

Steve frowned. "How do you mean?"

"She's solid. On the level." There was a pause,
and Squeaky's voice had taken on a lighter note
when he spoke again.

"What'd you *think* I meant? Like, do I find
her—attractive?"

Steve was suddenly glad that it was so dark.
"Do you?"

He could hear the grin in his partner's voice.

"Sure, I'd go for it. Can't say I'd mind slipping into those waters, she's one hot piece . . . How 'bout you?"

"Hadn't really thought about it."

Squeaky chuckled. "Yeah, *right,* hadn't really thought about it . . ."

Steve's light hit on a deck chart at the bottom of the flight, mounted to the wall. They were low enough for the chart to be relevant. He hurried down the last few steps, eager to get off the topic of Foster.

A quick study of the cryptic chart and Steve pointed to a blocked area in the mass of lines and squares. "The engine room should be here. One deck down."

He saw Squeaky nod in the reflected light and then they were moving again, down the empty stairwell to the engine level.

They picked up the pace as they reached the E deck, on more familiar ground now as they passed a small maintenance room filled with various machine parts and tools. Steve paused to look over their spare sets, and Squeaky checked the next room, a few feet ahead.

"Over here!"

Steve caught up and their beams joined at the main turbine that dominated the engine room. There were at least two other smaller generators, but there was no doubt which was the biggie; she was a beauty, an immense cylindrical machine that put every boat they'd ever worked to shame. The *Volkov* engineers must have been proud, and it appeared undamaged.

Steve hurried over, found the fuel boost pump, and primed it for action. He pressed the starter button and then scowled; nothing.

He turned his light towards his partner, talking fast. "Okay, let's hustle, Squeak. We gotta be facing into the wind when the storm hits. If we're in a typhoon without power to the rudder, we're dead."

Squeaky nodded and then smiled suddenly. He reached for the wiring harness, holding up the cut cords under Steve's flashlight.

Jesus, could that be all?

It was almost too good to be true, but it also seemed to be the only thing out of order. Squeaky started reconnecting the sliced cords with practiced ease as Steve moved around the massive turbine, checking switches and opening panels.

Everything was fine, no apparent damage to anything he could see. The saboteur obviously didn't know much about engines, had only severed a few connecting wires that could be fixed in minutes. It was better than they could have hoped.

"Almost done," said Squeaky, and Steve moved back to the starter as his partner connected the last wire, twisting the fibers together and pulling down the rubber sheath.

"Try it now."

Steve pressed the button and the rotor spun into action, filled the room with the rising hum of a well-maintained, powerful engine. Lights flickered on and he and Squeaky grinned at each other, squinting at the sudden brightness.

The *Volkov* had power.

■ ■ ■

The bridge suddenly surged to activity, undamaged monitors and instruments blinking on, consoles clicking and fans revving, overhead lights snapping away the gloom.

Everton smiled, feeling the *Volkov* come to life all around them. There was movement by the door and a video surveillance camera rose on its mount and swiveled in his direction.

"That's more like it," he said, glad that he'd had the foresight to hire such competent engineers. The bridge felt different suddenly, had gone from a dead room on a dead ship to the center of power for a sophisticated vessel; he could actually hear the decks beneath his feet switch on, the hum of hundreds of thousands of dollars worth of equipment reactivating—

—and there was a sound rising above the surging hum, like nothing he'd ever heard before—a strange, high-pitched squeal that seemed to grow in strength, swelling up from somewhere deep in the ship. Like a bird, screaming, like the howl of a machine in pain. Or rage . . .

What the devil—

Everton looked at Foster as the sound surged into the bridge, watched her cover her ears as the bizarre squeal became deafening, overwhelming—and then stopped, cut off abruptly as if it had never been.

"What the hell was that?" Foster asked, but Everton ignored her; obviously some damaged circuitry somewhere. The return of power had overloaded it and it had burnt out. An unusual sound, but no great mystery.

And apparently that's too vast a concept for our navigator to comprehend; what a surprise.

Everton picked up his walkie-talkie and clicked it on. "Good job, Baker. We're lit up like a pinball machine."

Baker didn't answer him directly, but he heard the engineer speak to his partner with the transmit button held. "Let's get the main engines running—" He cut off.

Everton walked to the port windows and looked down on the *Sea Star* as it moved into position to push the *Volkov*'s bow. Everything was going smoothly, perfectly—even the fog had thinned a bit. Richie had thrown down a line to Hiko and was directing Woods over the walkie while the Maori tied the hawser to the towing bit, just as they'd been ordered; Baker and his man had performed admirably, quickly. Foster, who had done nothing but poke at a few circuit boards and then declare the radio transmitter broken, was at least keeping her rather large mouth shut; he supposed it was the best he could hope for from her . . .

There was a rhythmic clicking hum from one of the consoles and Everton turned, wondering if the girl had actually managed to do something useful after all—but she was still digging through the charts, nowhere near the three screens that had booted themselves up in the center of the room.

She glanced at him, frowning, and walked across to the console. He joined her, not sure why he suddenly felt a bit—uncomfortable. The computers hadn't been on when the power had come back, he was sure of it. Now they were flipping through lines of data like slot machines, running through their programs at lightning speed.

"What the hell is going on?" Everton mumbled. The Cyrillic letters flashed past rapidly, almost as if the computers were searching for something.

Foster pressed a few buttons on the computer's keyboard, but nothing happened, at least that Everton could tell. He looked around the bridge absently and then back at the screens.

"Someone else is running this," said Foster nervously.

Everton frowned. "Looks like it's running itself."

"Computers don't run themselves," she said, and started tapping keys again.

Letters and numbers raced across the monitors, and Everton felt a cold fist tighten in his gut as they stopped suddenly, fixing on an icon of an anchor. The symbol blinked red, and Foster punched at more keys in desperation, accomplishing absolutely nothing.

Damn it, what now? Everton turned back to the windows, angry and suddenly quite nervous. Everything had been going so well—

—and he held his breath at the sound of heavy chain rattling outside, a sound he shouldn't, *couldn't* be hearing. Because the *Volkov*'s anchor was directly above the *Sea Star*'s position.

■ ■ ■

Richie held the walkie-talkie loosely and looked down on Hiko, standing on the deck of the *Star* and watching solemnly as the tug pushed the massive ship's bow into the direction of the coming wind. He was thinking idly about what a Maori would do with three million dollars; more tatts? Maybe there was a panel of tribal elders who decided shit like that, took money and passed it out to the peasants or something . . .

Whatever. Richie had already started making

plans; he was gonna set himself up good. He was gonna buy a new car, a Lamborghini, the kind you couldn't get in the States. He was gonna get a big ol' house in the Caribbean with a private beach and find one of those smiling island beauties to spend some time with, a nice girl with a tight body and big tits. They were gonna spend all day on the beach drinking and getting high and watching the waves, all night screwing their brains out on silk sheets—

There was a heavy rattling and Richie felt his brain freeze suddenly, even as he jerked his gaze down to the anchor well. He knew that sound.

No—

Time stretched and slowed, the next few seconds horribly clear, Richie helpless to stop it. He could only watch in dumb surprise as Hiko looked up, directly beneath the rattle of chain, his cool expression melting into one of shock and fear—

—as the *Volkov*'s anchor, seven to eight tons of iron and chain, let go of its mount and plummeted down.

· 10 ·

Foster looked away from the obstinate machine, frustrated and upset—and heard a tremendous, booming crash, her fears confirmed as Richie yelled from out on deck in panic.

"Fuck! Fuck—!"

His voice suddenly blared into the room over their walkies, high and breathless. "Emergency on main deck! The anchor hit the tug! Ripped a hole right through her!"

Everton pushed past her and they both ran for the door, hurrying out onto the deck and racing across to the port side. The captain shouted into his walkie as he ran.

"Baker! Baker, did you copy? Get up here!"

"Copy, I'm on my way—"

Foster rushed to the side and looked down, saw in a split second that the damage was irreparable. The *Sea Star* was going down fast, stern first, water spurting up through the gaping hole in the deck.

Hiko!

The Maori staggered across the tilting deck, blood pouring from a wound in his leg. Foster realized that he must have been almost right under the anchor; a thick, jagged chunk of wood decking had been driven deep into his right leg.

Hiko stopped, gripped the wood with a shaking hand, and pulled it out, face contorted in pain. He dropped the bloody, eight-inch shard to the deck and struggled on, trying to reach the railing.

Richie had grabbed a life preserver and marker, tossing them overboard even as Hiko collapsed to the deck, clutching his leg weakly. Foster looked around desperately, but there was only the one, the other preservers gone to the storm or the Russian crew.

Woods suddenly appeared from the *Sea Star*'s bridge, his face pale with terror. The helmsman saw the floating preserver and seemed to fix on it. He ran, stumbling across the slanting deck— and racing right past Hiko.

Hiko raised himself up, calling after him. "Woods, I can't make it! Where you goin'? Come back here, goddamn it—"

Woods didn't seem to hear him, didn't even pause, eyes wild and desperate. He dove off the sinking tug and struck out for the preserver, leaving Hiko behind.

Foster paced, searched for a place to dive in, but the angle was wrong, too close, she'd land on the sinking boat and break her neck. The anchor chain snapped from its eye suddenly, the heavy chain plunging to the deck and pushing the *Sea Star* down even faster.

She turned, started to run towards the fore——

—and saw Steve sprint out from the entry to below deck and run across to the *Volkov*'s railing.

"Woods!" Steve shouted, and Foster looked back, saw that the helmsman had reached the preserver and was watching the *Sea Star* go down, doing nothing to help the fallen crewman. Hiko had reached the railing; he kicked weakly, trailing blood as he tried to get higher, away from the rapidly rising water, his gaze bright with fear. The tug shifted suddenly, was upended— and then the railing was gone, too, Hiko's clutching hands disappearing beneath the churning sea.

* * *

Steve had just started to think about catching a short nap when Richie screamed emergency and Everton called for him to come up.

"Copy, I'm on my way!"

He handed the radio unit to Squeaky and started for the door of the humming room, pausing just long enough to give instructions.

"Stay tight! Any sign of trouble, don't play hero, get your ass outta here."

Squeaky gave him a thumbs-up and then Steve was running, down the dimly lit corridor and towards the stairs.

He took the steps in giant leaps, his thoughts racing. The anchor? The whole goddamn ship was electronic, everything hooked up to computers. It couldn't have happened, had to be a freak accident or—

—or someone else is on the ship, his mind whispered coolly, and Steve picked up speed, suddenly worried about more than a sinking tug. The *Sea Star* would have sunk anyway and it could have been an accident, sure—but wasn't it strange that the anchor had given way when the smaller ship was directly underneath?

He hit the A deck, all of the lights on and machinery humming as he raced through the corridors towards the exit to top deck. He noticed fleetingly that the *Volkov* felt like a different ship, now that it had power—different but somehow just as ominous as when it had been dark and silent . . .

No time to think. He burst through the hatch onto the open deck and ran for the railing. Foster was running towards him, but his gaze was fixed on the scene below.

"Woods!" he shouted, but the helmsman only floated there, his pale face turned towards the tug, watching blankly as the *Sea Star* slipped beneath the the waves, Hiko still holding on to the railing.

Steve was dumbstruck, unable to believe what he was seeing; a tense second passed, two, three—and Hiko broke through to the surface, paddling wildly, thrashing helplessly amidst pieces of shattered deck and bobbing debris. And Woods remained exactly where he was.

Chickenshit bastard!

Steve saw that Hiko wasn't going to make it and that Woods wasn't going to help. Without another thought, he jumped the railing and dove in.

The fall seemed to take forever, the deck easily three stories above the water. Steve had time to take a deep breath before he hit, plunged deep into the chilled ocean, and came up stroking smoothly towards Hiko.

The salt stung his eyes and it was cold, but he was close. He reached the struggling Maori in a few seconds.

"Relax, go limp," he breathed, and Hiko looked at him gratefully and stopped flailing, let his body relax as Steve wrapped an arm around his neck.

They started back for the *Volkov,* for the rope ladder that Steve had secured less than an hour before. Steve kicked strongly and swept with his right arm, concentrating on the ladder—but unable not to shoot a nasty glance at Woods, floating safely fifty feet away.

He looked back at the *Volkov,* saw that Richie had descended the ladder partway and was waiting to help, saw Foster's concerned face and Everton's scowling one looking down—and wondered again how the anchor had managed to release itself over the *Sea Star.*

We're not alone here—and whoever else is aboard doesn't want us to leave.

■ ■ ■

Hiko lay on the deck while the *Pakeha* gathered around nervously, casting tall shadows in the rapidly fading light. Foster leaned over him and studied his leg, Hiko trying not to wince when she gently touched the bleeding gash. The pain had been bad enough without the salt water, and blood still pulsed from the wound. He felt dizzy, though from blood loss or pain or just elation at being alive, he didn't know. He still had his *wa-*

haika, and he had survived; things could be worse.

Richie snapped his shotgun closed and paced anxiously in front of him. "That anchor didn't drop by itself. Someone else is on this ship."

Hiko had figured as much already. The *Volkov* felt bad to him, had felt bad the second he'd seen her. He could tell that the others felt the same way, and wondered why they continued to deny their fear; it didn't take Maori blood to know when something was fucked up. The Russian ship was haunted, it was *kino*. Someone hiding in it had tried to kill him and had almost succeeded.

He looked up at Foster and smiled a little at her worried expression.

"I'll be all right," he said, but she wasn't going to hear it.

"Not without stitches. We gotta find a sick bay."

Steve handed her a knife and she cut open Hiko's pant leg, revealing the oozing wound amidst the deep designs of his *moko*. He frowned; there would be a scar. The wood from the deck had messed up a beautiful design, hours of detailed work lost.

Foster reached up and tugged at his belt, releasing the buckle and sliding it from underneath him. Hiko glanced around uncertainly.

"What are you doing? Hey . . ."

Foster shot him a glance and then looped the leather above his knee, tightening it. A tourniquet. Hiko looked away, embarrassed. Maybe he *did* need stitches; he was still dizzy and had thought for a moment that she was reaching for something else entirely.

"That coulda been me, ya know," said Woods to no one in particular.

Hiko focused on Woods, felt a slow anger kindle in his belly as the helmsman pulled off his wet tee and dropped it to the deck. Richie reached into his bag and produced a dry shirt, tossing it to Woods but not looking to see if he caught it.

Hiko glanced over at Steve, saw the same contempt on the engineer's wet face as he stared at Woods. The man was a spider, all right; Hiko hated spiders.

Steve picked up a walkie-talkie and clicked it on; before he could speak, his partner's voice crackled out.

"Steve, Squeaky. What the hell happened?"

"The tug's gone, Squeak. Sunk."

"Well, that sucks."

Hiko nodded to himself; well put.

"How you doin'?" Steve asked.

"I'm okay. This ship is automated, everything runs itself—"

"Wrong. Somebody is still on board, they sank the tug. Bolt the door and don't let anybody in there. We'll be right down."

"Copy that," said Squeaky, and Hiko could hear a sudden wariness in his voice. Wariness, but no surprise.

Steve clicked off the unit and turned, addressing all of them. "Let's divide up into two groups and root 'em out."

Foster nodded. "I agree with Steve."

Captain Everton frowned, raised his voice. "Wait a minute, I'm still captain here."

Steve met his gaze evenly. "You were captain of the *Sea Star*. Which just sank."

Hiko propped up on his elbows, watched as the two men glared at each other. He didn't like Everton particularly, and decided that he would back Steve, if it came to that. Everton hadn't saved him from the *moana*.

"Listen to me, Baker—I'm still ranking officer, and I'm willing to overlook what happened between us. Do we have a problem with that?"

Steve shrugged, said nothing, and Everton turned towards the rest of them, looking angry but self-satisfied.

"Richie, Woods, go down to the engine room and back up Squeaky; Baker, Foster, and I will take Hiko to the medical bay and dress that wound. Let's move."

With that, he turned and walked away, headed for the foredeck. Hiko sat up, deciding that he definitely didn't like the man—and he could tell from the looks on the others' faces that they didn't, either. Even Woods seemed unhappy with the order, and that made the captain lower than low in Hiko's book . . .

He let Foster and Steve help him to his feet, his leg already numb below the tight belt, and found himself wishing that he'd flown home after all. He didn't like this ship, he didn't trust Everton, and he wanted nothing more than to be on dry land, away from this terrible mess.

Facing one's fears was definitely not all it was cracked up to be.

▪ || ▪

Everton led the way to the stairwell, noting that at least some of the lights were working. It was still dim, the corridor deeply shadowed but decidedly empty. He shone the flashlight into the darker corners, Foster and Baker supporting the wounded man behind him.

Everton kept a blank expression as they reached the stairs, but it was difficult to maintain. Woods and the two deckhands hadn't openly defied him, at least not yet—but with Foster and Baker both trying to undermine his authority, he felt his control slipping. Splitting the troublesome pair away from the others should put an end to it, although suffering such disrespect didn't sit well with him—and after he'd offered a more-than-generous percentage, too. It was unbelievable.

The landing light was on, but the steps before

them were still dark. He directed the beam down and led the threesome forward, wondering if their stowaway was likely to try a more direct attack than through a computer. Sinking the *Sea Star* had been a rather cowardly form of terrorism—he suspected that the perpetrator of such an act would stay hidden, not wanting to confront an armed crew. He'd stay on his guard, though, until the intruder was found; he wasn't about to take any unnecessary risks, not anymore. There was too much at stake.

The surveillance cameras were working, panning back and forth all through the A corridor and another in the well; practically every inch of the ship looked to be covered. They could use them to hunt down whoever else was on board, once they'd regrouped. He hoped that Foster could at least manage to do *that* much with a computer; she'd certainly failed in saving the *Sea Star*—

A soft sound, somewhere in the dark ahead. Everton froze, but it was already gone, too slight to even resonate in the empty stairwell. He aimed the beam of his flashlight over the railing, but saw only more steps. A light clattering noise, metallic.

He glanced back, but it was obvious that the others hadn't heard it; the two hotheads were concentrating on getting Hiko down the steps. Everton decided that it was nothing, probably debris falling; the *Volkov* wasn't exactly in top shape. Besides, it wasn't loud enough to have come from anything as big as a human being; maybe the Russians had rats.

His light fell across a mounted wall chart at the bottom of the flight and he stepped down quickly to examine it. The A deck had been mostly small laboratories, at least from what he could tell, but this chart seemed to be more diversified; the brightly colored squares indicated multiple environments.

Foster joined him, studying the map. "I can't tell the sick bay from the mess hall. Any suggestions?"

Everton wasn't sure, but he wasn't going to let her know that. The fact that she'd bothered to ask meant that she recognized his greater experience—and that she was still willing to be led.

He pointed to a midsized block of blue squares, careful to speak as though he were open to her take on the matter. "Probably here—or here," he said, indicating a green pattern next to the blue. "We'll have to look."

Foster nodded and went back to help Baker. Everton smiled inwardly; Foster seemed to think she was his peer somehow; he could use that. Perhaps it would work on Baker, too—if giving commands didn't work, he'd try the we're-all-in-this-together approach. It was ridiculous, a captain having to bother with such things, but he needed them to get the *Volkov* through the storm. He'd simply have to compromise, at least until they reached safe waters.

He pushed the unsealed hatch open, revealing another dim corridor that stretched off in both directions. He waited for the others to catch up and they moved into the hall, headed for what he hoped would be sick bay.

Get our man stitched up, lay out a plan for capturing whoever attacked us—and get back to what's important here. Taking our find in and collecting our due . . .

No one had better try to stop him. He'd been through too much already to let anyone stand in his way; the *Volkov* was his, and he'd do whatever it took to keep it.

■ ■ ■

The door to the engine room was bolted, the shotgun was in easy reach, and Woods and Richie were coming—but Squeaky was still deeply uneasy. It was creepy, being alone in unfamiliar territory when there was some Russian crazy running around. And it didn't help that every goddamn time he moved, the video camera bolted over the door tracked after him; rigged up to some kind of a motion sensor, which was interesting and all, but it still felt weird. Like someone was watching him.

He had rummaged through his sack and found a half pack of cigarettes, left over from the last time he swore he'd never smoke again. Actually, it had only been a few days and he'd already cheated, but who the fuck cared? Steve was always getting on his case about it, but Steve wasn't here—and besides, he was tense.

He lit another and propped himself up on a stool, holding the walkie in one hand and looking at the main turbine. That was a lot of horses, no shit; the smooth hum of the impressive machine was soothing, relaxing to his nerves.

He was thinking that he'd buy his own shop with his share of the salvage money, one that was outfitted for cars, boats, maybe even small planes—state of the art all the way. He could hire the best mechanics and supervise everything personally. He'd always liked mechanical stuff, even as a kid; there was a certain satisfaction that came with tooling around engines, making them run the way they were supposed to. He didn't want to give that up just because he could afford to.

He grinned, reminded of an old joke. *Maybe I'll run a charity clinic, free service for all the ladies—"Let me look under your hood and get your motor running—and I'll fix your engine, too," something like that—*

Someone was watching him.

Squeaky's smile faded and he turned slowly, gaze darting around the room. The video camera was still on him, but it hadn't felt like that, hadn't felt like that at all . . .

Nobody. Nothing but machines, and he decided that he was definitely in need of a stiff drink; he'd have to hit Woods up for a belt, that weaselly dork always carried, and where *were* they, anyway? Leaving him down here to get all paranoid when there was a nut on the loose; it was practically inhumane.

Squeaky took another drag off his smoke and wondered what Steve would do with his share; maybe they could go in together, that would be all right—

A scuttling movement behind him. Squeaky wheeled around, searched the row of generators for the source, his heart pounding and eyes wide. Nothing, he couldn't see anything, but the sound persisted. Like a spider with metal legs, skittering.

"Hey! Somebody there?" His voice cracked.

His gaze was caught by a sudden movement between two of the generators, near a thick bundle of cords and cables that ran through an access hole in the deck. The tail end of an electrical cord disappeared through the hole, as if jerked down by unseen hands.

He stubbed out his smoke and put down the walkie, still scared but not as bad as when he'd first heard that weird noise. It couldn't be a person, unless they were four feet tall or could breathe fuel oil; there wasn't room under the deck for anything else.

So what made that noise? And where did the cord go?

Had to be a mechanical problem; one of the cords had gotten caught on something, that was all—maybe hooked onto a rotor or some such. Squeaky picked up the flashlight and clicked it on, walking over to the bundle of cables and feeling like an idiot.

Terrific, great—leave me alone for ten minutes and I turn into a fuckin' mouse. Squeaky, that's me...

He stepped up to the access hole and shone the light down, seeing only the thick cables that led off to one side, distributing power to the ship. The hole was just big enough for the bundle, maybe three feet across, and packed to all sides with the heavily insulated cords.

He crouched down and stuck his hand into the mass, spreading the cables as far as they would go. He squeezed himself forward, surprised at how easily they parted; he'd be able to get a pretty good look after all—

—and the cables tightened suddenly, trapping his arms against his body.

"What the fuck—!"

He struggled against them, terrified, unable to get free. The cords pulled tight, tighter—and jerked him down through the hole and into the darkness, before he even had time to scream.

■ ■ ■

Woods was dogging his heels like a scared woman; every time Richie stopped, the skinny blond tripped all over himself not to run into him. Richie thought it was pretty funny, actually; he'd stopped suddenly a couple of times just to watch the man dance.

They were on C deck, and it was dark. Not pitch black, they had passed a couple of overheads, but the corridors seemed to be randomly lit; for every lamp on, there were three or four off. It made for strange patterns, tricking out Richie's perspective so the halls seemed to stretch and condense in front of them.

Woods had only protested their little side trip once, but Richie had set him straight. If they were gonna be wandering around in hostile territory, they needed to be ready for anything; he'd just told Junior that he was free to go down to the engine room solo if he didn't like it. Woods had shut up quick after that, and had been breathing down his neck ever since.

They'd already passed several storerooms with bedding and uniforms and shit like that, not to mention a couple of computer rooms that had been totally trashed. Richie knew they were close; the layout of the *Volkov* was similar to ships he'd heard about back in AIT.

Research vessel, my black ass. Researching on weapons development, more like it, out here, all quiet like . . .

Richie stopped in front of a heavy door, and

Woods caught himself about an inch from running into him, his face pale and slick in the cool, shadowy hall. Richie smirked and opened the door, shining his flashlight into the room.

He felt a slow grin spread across his face and took in the sight, deeply satisfied at what he saw. Racks of AK-47s and banana clips; Rocket Propelled Grenade Launchers, 58.3-millimeter thermite grenades, they looked like, and the Russian equivalent of a 16D antitank launcher to go with 'em. No way a spy ship wasn't gonna be equipped to the teeth, he *knew* it.

"Weapons locker," he said, and stepped inside, Woods close behind.

He snapped on the lights, still grinning, and reached for one of the AK-47s, checking the bore and nodding happily. Chromed and smooth, hadn't been fired with any of that corrosive shit that the Ruskies had been so fond of for so long . . .

"Is that . . . is that an AK-47?" Woods asked anxiously.

"Yeah. Kicks all ass over an M-16, Woodsy— we're talking rapid-fire capability, high muzzle velocity . . . Got a short sighting radius, but you don't even need to aim one a' these babies, just point and squeeze."

He tossed the rifle to the helmsman and watched him fumble with it, then turned and picked up a munitions pack, handing it to the other man. "Let's load up."

Richie fell to the work with a vengeance, stuffing Woods's pack with every clip on the rack; each curved black mag held thirty. The RPGs went in too, since the grenade launchers only held two missiles—he could see that they were finned, meant a nice, flat trajectory and slow rotation; excellent fuckin' accuracy. He found a couple of sets of night vision goggles, not as good as a starlight scope but better than nothing; they went in on top.

He stood up and looked around, nodding. They'd cleared the locker out, but there was another hatch at the end of the room that probably led to more. Woods had six AK-47s slung across his back and the grenade launcher sagging off one shoulder.

"C'mon, Richie, that's enough."

Richie shook his head, picked up the last AK-47, and slammed a clip home. "You can never be too rich, too thin, or too well armed," he said, and opened the hatch. A stairwell, dark and empty.

Richie pulled a joint out of his breast pocket and lit up, held the first toke in until his brain started to scream for air. He exhaled slowly, feeling at ease for the first time since the whole anchor incident. There was a watcher on this boat, maybe more than one; those goddamn video cameras all over, the back of his neck going cold every time one found him, fuckin' with him—

—*but now we're cookin' with gas; ain't no commie bastard gonna get the drop on me, no way no how* . . .

"Where ya goin'? Let's get outta here, Richie."

Woods sounded like a cartoon. Richie took another hit and started down the dark stairs. Squeaky could wait, at least until Richie had scoped out the available firepower.

He was a man with a mission. And God help the Russians, 'cause he was through bein' fucked with.

· 12 ·

The sick bay wasn't where Everton had proposed, but it was close. Foster threw open the door and found the lights, the bright fluorescents chasing away the shadows and showing them a gleaming white medical lab. There were wide lockers, gurneys, stainless tables—it seemed to be one of the only places on the ship so far that hadn't been wrecked.

Foster walked in cautiously, Everton, Steve, and Hiko right behind. She heard the mounted camera in one upper corner swivel towards them and glanced up, felt a chill run through her; there were surveillance cams everywhere on the *Volkov,* probably standard equipment on a vessel like this—but she couldn't help feeling like they were being tracked, their every move studied. Whoever had dropped the anchor on the *Sea Star* obviously had the skills to do it, too; they'd blocked the bridge console from them easily enough . . .

They all stood for a moment, listening, but the lab seemed empty of life, as empty as the rest of the ship.

But not empty, either—it's like a ship of ghosts, invisible but always watching. We can't see them, but they're here with us now, sliding between us, examining us, touching us . . .

She shook off the feeling and walked to a counter of drawers and cabinets that lined one side of the room, opposite the locker bank. Steve and Everton helped Hiko to one of the examining tables while she pulled open drawers, found gauze and boxes of rubber gloves. She crouched down in front of a cabinet and got lucky on the first—swabs, bottles of disinfectant, and suture kits. She grabbed up an armful and walked across to where Hiko lay, Everton leaning on the table. Steve was rummaging around for dry clothes in one of the lockers.

The Maori deckhand watched stoically as she undid the makeshift tourniquet and wiped the nasty wound with an iodine solution. She threaded the surgical needle and took a deep breath.

"This is gonna hurt, Hiko."

He shrugged. "Just get on with it."

Steve had found a set of scrubs and stepped behind a medical curtain to change. Foster hesitated with the needle, unable to help a quick look as he slipped out of his wet pants. From where she sat, she could see one well-muscled thigh, the heavy, wet material pushing down . . .

Jesus, am I in high school again? Foster turned back to the work at hand, embarrassed at herself. She pierced the ragged edge of flesh and pushed through as gently as she could. Hiko didn't even flinch.

"You've got a high pain threshold," she said quietly.

"I usually do it myself," he answered. She couldn't quite tell if he was kidding, but looking at the depth of the tattoo work he'd had done, she thought probably not.

Everton had produced another handful of peanuts from somewhere and looked over at her, speaking conversationally as he munched.

"Foster—what are you gonna do with your three million?"

She concentrated on making another stitch across the deep gash, fully aware that the captain was trying to make nice and not particularly interested. "I don't have it yet."

Everton continued. "Say you do. Seriously, what would you do?"

She shrugged; she had nothing to say to the man, and in truth, she hadn't thought about it yet.

Hiko obviously had. "I'd open a school."

Steve walked out from behind the curtain in a loose set of surgical scrubs. He tossed another set to Hiko, smiling. "A school?"

Hiko nodded. "*Kura Kaupapa*. You know, for little kids. Teach them to read and write Maori, that sort of thing."

Everton worked to keep it going. "What about you, Baker?"

Steve was opening the wide medical lockers, checking the contents. "I dunno. I don't have any attachments; always loved the sea . . ." He paused, then smiled. "I'd buy an island."

Foster considered that, finishing a third stitch. "Interesting idea. Does it have a beach?"

"Yeah. Nice white sand."

Foster smiled. "And a house?"

"With a thatched roof, overlooking a lagoon."

Hiko grinned. "When are you guys getting married? Ow! Foster, take it easy!"

Foster looked over at Steve, saw him watching her thoughtfully as he reached for another locker. Interesting indeed . . .

He pulled the handle up, and quite suddenly, all hell broke loose.

■ ■ ■

Steve dove for cover as a shadowy figure opened fire from inside the deep locker, the popping sound of an automatic rifle shattering the stillness of the lab.

Steve spun, saw Foster push Hiko off the table and Everton hit the deck as the Russian strafed the lab with the AK-47. Glass doors blew into fragments, the metal table where Hiko had lain pierced by ringing bullets.

He saw Everton's shotgun propped up against the base of the lockers and scrambled for it, reaching it just as the Russian jumped down, still firing wildly. Steve saw that a gas mask covered his head, saw the rifle pivot towards him—

—and the click of an empty weapon, the clip out of rounds.

Steve launched himself at the attacker, raised the butt of the shotgun and drove it into the Russian's chest, knocking him back into the locker. The crash of the man's head against metal was loud in the sudden silence and the Russian slumped, his body limp.

Steve grabbed the boots of the still figure and pulled him out onto the floor. Guy was a light-weight, couldn't weigh more than 120 or so—short, too.

He looked over his shoulder, saw Hiko and Foster turn stunned faces towards him, Everton looking out from behind the examination table behind them. Amazingly, no one had been hit.

Steve reached for the gas mask, adrenaline still coursing through his body.

Fucker tried to kill *me!*

He yanked at the mask, ready to beat the shit out of the man if he so much as twitched—

—and blinked, surprised. "He" was a woman, and an attractive one at that. Her fragile features were smooth, a few loose strands of long, dirty blond hair framing a pale, heart-shaped face.

Steve dropped the mask, turned to the others, and saw the same dismay he felt. He wasn't a chauvinist or anything, but a woman acting so violently, Russian or no—

Why? What the hell is going on here?

Maybe she'd be able to tell them when she woke up. Assuming she knew any English, assuming that she was sane—and assuming that she woke up at all.

■ ■ ■

J. W. Woods, Jr., couldn't get drunk. His hip flask was over half empty and he seemed to be sweating it out as fast as he put it down; every inch of his body dripped and ran with clammy rivers of sweat, as it had ever since he'd set foot on this forsaken ship.

He wished the *Sea Star* were still afloat, wished

it desperately. He wished that he could be with the captain instead of here in the dark, echoing room that Richie had led them to below the weapons locker. He wished a lot of things, but most of all that the whiskey would do its job and give him a little peace.

Everyone thought he was a pussy, fine, whatever—but he didn't want to die, and he didn't want to be alone on a ship where there was an insane Russian trying to kill them all.

I'm a survivor, that's all; what's wrong with wanting to be alive? I coulda gone down with the Star, *but does anyone even care? Crazy, all of 'em: they call* me *pussy and they're off trying to get themselves killed, like that makes them "brave"...*

Everton was the only one who showed him any respect; he should've insisted on staying with the captain, he was a *leader*, he was strong. Instead, he was off with a gun-crazy deckhand when Everton had told them to go help Squeaky. They shouldn't be here.

Richie was still smoking marijuana and poking around with his flashlight, like they had all the time in the world. His beam fell across a rack of some kind, loaded with what looked like—missiles?

Richie aimed his light at the open space beyond, the beam illuminating another missile, lined up at the base of some kind of tube. In fact, there was a whole set of tubes, some small, some much bigger.

Launch tubes?

Richie's voice was deliriously upbeat as the light flickered back to the first missile. "This thing is armed—tactical short range, surface to air . . . beautiful!''

"I'm thrilled," said Woods. He raised his flask and took a healthy slug. "Can we go now?"

"In a minute." Richie started poking around again, playing his light along the floor.

Woods took another swig, watching hopelessly as Richie studied the mess that his flashlight revealed. It looked like someone had been down here taking missiles apart; there were piles of metal shells stacked all around, pieces of the dismantled bombs all over.

"Hey, Woods, what do you make of this?"

"Dunno," he answered sullenly. He sighed, slipped the flask back into his hip pocket, and raised his flashlight to join Richie's. Maybe if he helped, they could get out of here sooner. He wanted to get back to the captain, get somewhere that had *light*.

He followed Richie across the dark room towards the launch tubes, not sure what the man was even looking for and not really caring. The flashlight was slick in his grasp. He switched hands, wiped his palms against his shirt, and waited for Richie to explain what they were seeing.

Richie's light passed over some kind of platform at the bottom of one of the really big launch tubes. There was a cable that ran from the inside rail of the tube to the platform itself. There was a metal chair welded and braced to it, looped with what looked like seat belts.

"Looks like an ejection seat, some kinda escape vehicle," said Richie. He picked up a small box next to the chair that had connecting cords running to a panel in the wall. He studied it, nodding slowly.

"Launch buttons. Cool."

Woods had to stifle an urge to tell Richie to hurry up; he didn't want to piss the guy off, he might—leave him there, alone. Woods swallowed, turned away from the tubes to see what else he could find.

He ran his flashlight along the opposite wall and froze, a fresh layer of sweat suddenly oozing out of his pores. One of the *Volkov*'s watertight hatches was illuminated by the shaking beam; it had been smashed in from the outside, buckled into its frame. There were multiple welts in the thick steel, each the size of a man's fist.

Strong, whoever did that was—had to have had a battering ram, no way a man's that strong.

His beam dropped to the base of the door where there was a puddle of thick, brownish red liquid. At least three or four feet across, and still very wet.

"Hey, Richie—" Woods's voice shook and he swallowed again, as Richie turned his light to the tiny lake and stopped there.

"That's a lot of blood," he finished weakly, and reached again for his flask, suddenly quite desperate not to feel the terror that had taken over his entire body. He closed his eyes and drank long, not stopping until he started to choke on the sweet, fiery relief.

·13·

Everton helped Foster lift the unconscious woman into a chair, feeling deeply relieved. They'd caught their Russian, it was all over. She had tried to kill them, she had dropped an anchor on their tug—she was obviously insane, and that meant that she wasn't competent to claim the *Volkov*. No court would dispute it, and he had witnesses.

The woman slumped into the chair, and Everton looked over to see Hiko digging through the waist satchel that Baker had taken off the Russian. He pulled out empty food packets, half a pack of Russian cigarettes, matches—

Everton smiled to himself. An entire ship to herself and she was running around like some kind of commando, gas mask and all, lugging her little bag of necessities and an automatic rifle. He wondered if she'd murdered her shipmates before or after trashing all the radios . . .

Hiko pulled out a dark hand-sized object, two, three of them. There was a flat digital panel hooked up to a small circuit board . . .

Everton suddenly realized what it meant, but Foster beat him to the warning.

Hiko, picking up a canister, "What's that? Hairspray?"

"Careful, Hiko," he said sharply. "Thermite grenades."

Hiko frowned. "What?"

Baker nodded at the explosives. "One of those goes off, it'll burn a hole right through the deck."

Hiko shook his head and very carefully started putting the grenades back into the satchel. "What was she gonna do? Blow up the ship?"

Everton wanted to laugh. *Proof, as if we needed any more! Crazy, mad as a Russian hatter!*

Baker picked up a walkie and called to his partner. "Squeaky. Come in, Squeaky, do you copy?"

Silence, and Everton saw Baker frown, saw Hiko and Foster exchange a worried look.

"Squeaky, c'mon, don't play games."

Still nothing. Baker's man had apparently wandered off without his radio; Everton scowled. As if they didn't have enough to contend with.

Baker depressed the transmit again. "Richie, Woods, come back."

Richie answered, his voice crackling brightly. "Steve, this ship's got a missile room—"

Baker's temper flashed. "I don't give a shit about missiles, Richie! My best friend's in the engine room and he's not answering—now, get your ass down there!"

The deckhand sounded put out that Baker wasn't impressed. "We hear ya, we hear ya."

Baker continued, glancing over at the unconscious Russian nervously. "And just so you know, we've got a crewman up here who emptied an assault rifle on us, so keep your eyes open; meet me in the engine room in five minutes."

Everton frowned, but decided to let it slide. Baker wanted to play captain, fine; the mystery had already been solved, it was highly unlikely that there could be *two* Russian mental cases running around, and the *Volkov* was still his. If the other engineer had gotten himself lost, well, that was *his* problem. With any luck, Baker would do the same; unlikely, but one could always hope . . .

The Russian woman moaned softly and rolled her head back, starting to come to. Baker picked up the shotgun and they all focused on the groaning woman, tensing for action in case she went off again.

Everton reached into his pocket for his bag of peanuts and settled in for the show.

■ ■ ■

Richie moved through the dark corridor of C deck, Woods close behind, both of them sporting AK-47s and edging cautiously forward. The stairs should be around here somewhere; Richie had kind of lost his sense of direction, and the way Woods was staggering along, he'd kind of lost his, too.

Place is a fuckin' maze, he thought bitterly. *Goddamn Russians with their goddamn spy ships. Probably set up like this on purpose, to confuse people . . .*

He figured if they just kept going, stuck to the main corridor, it'd circle back around to a stairwell eventually. There was another turn ahead and they moved on, Richie still thinking about what Steve had said. Russian crewmen with rifles, Squeaky missing—the poor sap must've unbolted the door and gotten himself shot. It was a goddamn shame.

Just try it on us, Ruskies; we've locked and loaded, gonna blow you a new asshole . . .

They turned the corner and stopped, staring down at the mess that littered the dim hall. Thick cables had been ripped out of the ceiling, and were strewn like spider webs crisscrossing the corridor.

"What happened here?" Woods whispered, slurring his words together.

Richie shook his head. "Somebody doesn't like electricity."

They stepped carefully through the snaking cables, Richie noticing that the corridor turned again up ahead, to the left. There was a hatch at the end of this hall, though; maybe it led to stairs.

They reached the hatch and Richie stepped forward, trying to make sense of the sign next to it in the dim light. Russian was weird-looking, mixing up perfectly good letters with shit that didn't make sense—

Something streaked up in front of him and hovered, insectlike, an inch from his face.

Fuck—

He stumbled backwards, nearly tripped over Woods. A bright light flashed on from the buzzing thing, blinding him.

Richie batted it with his rifle, too startled to think straight. The barrel connected with metal, solid, and the thing fell, thrashing wildly, humming and buzzing as it twisted across the floor.

He aimed at it, fired—and it stopped moving, the light and sound cutting off instantly.

Jesus H. Christ!

What *was* it? Richie stared down at the metal—*thing,* unable to figure out what it was he was looking at. Like a giant insect, made out of machine parts. Less than a foot across, winged, a lens on the oblong body where the light had come from—

It's a robot! A fuckin' 'droid!

Richie prodded at it with the barrel of his weapon, but it didn't move. His bullets had severed a twisting cable that jutted out of its back, and he realized that he must have cut off its power.

He looked down at the cable, saw that it snaked down the corridor to their left, trailing off into darkness. Richie crouched down and picked up the 'droid, amazed at how light it was in spite of the obvious fact that it was made out of metal.

"What is it? It smells like dog shit, Richie."

Richie stared down at the strange, insectoid body in his hand, thoughts racing. "It's robotics, man. High-tech robotics."

Woods sounded as awed as Richie felt. "What's it for?"

Richie blew out slowly, shook his head. "I don't know. Never seen anything like it, look at this engineering . . . With shit like this, how'd the Russians lose the Cold War? C'mon."

They both raised their rifles and started down the hall to their left, following the severed cable that would take them to its source of power. Richie grinned to himself, eager to see more and feeling wired out of his skull with excitement and curiosity.

So this is what they've been up to out here: fanfuckin'-tastic! No wonder they don't want us to see this . . .

Reminded of the enemy, he clutched his weapon tighter and they moved off into the darkness, Richie leading the way.

■ ■ ■

Nadia was dreaming, a dark and terrible dream of blue fire, and there was distant pain, in her head and chest. It seemed to go on for a long time, this dream, but the pain grew stronger, sharper—and the dream faded out like an old, ugly memory, the surface of reality rushing towards her like a light . . .

She opened her eyes groggily and there *was* light. Bright light, shining down from above. And people, the people who had done this thing. Real people.

Panic flushed through her, panic and a terror so great that she almost couldn't breathe.

"The lights, no! Shut off the power, it needs power! You have to listen, I didn't know you were real before, you've made a terrible mistake!"

There was a woman leaning over her, a pretty woman with a worried expression. The woman babbled gently at her in a foreign language, the words soothing but wrong, all wrong.

Nadia took a deep breath, concentrated.

"EE-zee," she said. "Easy"? English? Oh, thank God! Nadia *knew* English, she'd had to in order to work with the American astronauts.

The woman spoke again. "We're American, you know, U.S.A.? English?"

Nadia pointed at the lights, finding the words quickly. "Power! Turn off the power, shut down the ship! You're all in danger!"

They all looked at her and she looked back, searching for comprehension in their pale faces. A young, dark-haired man in scrubs with a shotgun. An older man with a sailing cap. The pretty young woman in a reddish shirt, and there was another, he looked Polynesian, Maori perhaps.

"What's she going on about?" The Maori, asking the others as if she weren't even there.

The dark-haired man shook his head. "Beats me. I'm going after Squeaky."

What's "Squeaky"?

The woman looked at the young man with concern. "Be careful. Meet up with us on the bridge."

The man met her deep gaze and nodded, chambering a round in the shotgun. Nadia saw that they were lovers, and felt her stomach knot with sadness.

"See you on the bridge," he said, and left the sick bay.

Nadia closed her eyes and raised a shaking hand to her head, searching for the words that would make them understand. Already they acted as though she were crazy—

—*and why wouldn't they? You tried to kill*

*them, you probably look like hell, haven't slept
or bathed in days.*

She opened her eyes, saw the older man in the
American captain hat and the Maori moving
closer to where she sat, expressions tight with
suspicion. The captain held a crinkly bag, and as
he neared her, she smelled roasted nuts.

Without thinking, she snatched for the bag,
mouth watering. The captain pulled away, ex-
changing a look with the woman.

Nadia felt her eyes well up. "I have not eaten
in three days," she said softly.

The captain frowned, then handed the bag
over. Nadia couldn't even thank him, she was
too overcome by animal need. She stuffed a
great handful into her mouth, hardly chewing the
rich, salty peanuts.

She felt her stomach clench, but it didn't reject
the nourishment. She nodded thankfully, could
already feel her exhausted mind clearing as the
protein hit her system.

"What is your name?" The woman, her voice
gentle.

The captain spoke before she could answer.
"What happened on this ship? Where's the rest
of your crew?"

Nadia swallowed, listened to the words, and
looked between the captain and the woman, desperate to say the right thing and make them understand.

She focused on the captain, their leader. He
was the one she had to convince.

"Dead. All dead. You must shut off the
power. It needs power to move through the
ship."

"*What* needs power?"

How could she explain? Nadia fixed her gaze on his and realized there was no word for the thing.

"It," she said again, and pointed upwards. "From the MIR."

The woman studied her seriously. "The space station?"

Nadia nodded and stuffed another handful of peanuts in her mouth, chewing around the word. "Yes!"

The captain rolled his eyes in exasperation. "Jesus, we got us a—"

Nadia frowned, swallowed. She didn't know the word.

Froot-caik?

The woman looked at him, upset. "Hold on, Captain—"

The captain waved a dismissive hand at her, and she didn't need to know the exact meaning, she could see it in his face, hear it in the way he spoke. "She's a fucking nut-bag! Look at her!"

Nadia realized that he wouldn't hear her, that his ears were closed. The leader of these people thought her insane, wouldn't listen until his crew was dead—or worse than dead, and with the power on, that wouldn't be far away.

She had to get out, try to turn off the engines before it was too late.

Nadia took a deep breath, and when the captain turned back to her she sprang at him, lacing her fingers together and bashing at the side of his head.

He fell against a cabinet and to the floor and she was running, sprinting from the medical lab and into the corridor, praying that there was still time.

• 14 •

The Russian jumped out of her chair and hit Everton with both hands, hard, dropping him. Before Foster even had time to blink, the woman ran out of the sick bay.

The captain was down, Hiko couldn't run— she realized that there was no one else and took off after her, reaching for the .32 pistol in her pocket that Steve had given her a seeming eternity before.

She hit the hallway, heard glass breaking. She whipped around, saw the woman reach into a mounted case on the wall at the end of the corridor and grab a fire ax. Then she was running again, around a corner and out of sight.

"Ah, *shit*."

Foster sprinted after her, rounded the same corner, and saw an open hatch, leading to a set of stairs different from the ones they'd used to get Hiko to the sick bay; these started on the B deck. The woman could only have gone down.

There was light, at least. Foster gripped the pistol tightly and ran down the steps, three at a time. She turned at the midflight landing—

—and saw the Russian stopped at the hatch to the C deck, pushing desperately at the thick metal. It seemed to be blocked from the other side. Bits of electrical cord littered the floor.

Foster stopped midway down the steps and pointed the .32, struggling to catch her breath. "Hold it right there!"

The woman turned, saw the weapon, and held very still, her face pale and afraid. Foster motioned at the ax.

"Drop it!"

The woman lowered the ax slowly, then dropped it to the floor, the blade clattering heavily against the metal landing. She sank down beside it, looking as deeply upset and exhausted as Foster had ever seen another person look. It was as if the life had drained out of her, her very will to live suddenly gone.

Foster edged closer, the battered pistol still trained on her, but she couldn't imagine the pitiful woman even standing up again, let alone attacking. The knuckles of her right hand dripped blood slowly.

"What were you going to do with that?" Foster asked.

The woman turned a pleading, anxious gaze up to her. "You don't understand," she said softly.

"I understand that you just hit my captain," Foster said, and before she could stop herself, whispered under her breath, "something I've wanted to do for a long time ..."

The woman was trembling, terrified and miserable, and Foster lowered the gun, took a deep breath, and put it back in her pocket. If the Russian was faking this, she deserved an Oscar; she honestly seemed to be having some kind of a breakdown and no longer seemed violent at all. Foster raised both her hands and stepped forward, now only a few feet from her.

"My name is Kelly Foster. I'm a navigator."

The woman gazed at her warily, then said in a small, hopeful voice, "I am Nadia. Nadia Vinogradova, chief science officer."

There was a clatter down the steps behind them and Everton ran down the stairs, Hiko limping along behind him. Both had firearms, both trained on Nadia.

Foster took a calculated risk and turned towards the two men, leaving herself wide open for attack. She looked at Everton seriously.

"That isn't necessary. You too, Hiko. Put it down."

She turned back to the shuddering woman, keeping her hands in sight and her voice low and easy, her words simple. "Nadia, once again. Slowly. Where is your crew?"

Nadia seemed to realize that this was her chance to explain. She blew out slowly, met Foster's gaze. "I told you. Dead or deserted."

Everton scoffed loudly. "Deserted? In this storm, three hundred crewmen? Bullshit."

Foster shot him a look. "Captain, please ..."

Nadia went on, frowning in concentration. "Eight days ago, during a transmission from the MIR space station, something came onto the ship. We thought our transmitter and receivers were malfunctioning, so we shut them down. It took control of computers, scanned all—information. Language, encyclopedias, medical data. It was learning."

"Learning what?" Foster asked, crouching down in front of her.

"How to—kill us. My captain, Alexi, and I were the last to survive. We cut their cables, smashed them."

Foster frowned. " 'Them'? You just said 'it.' Who's *them*?"

Nadia said a word in Russian, her face crumpling as she spoke, eyes tearing and mouth turning down. Then in English.

"Machines," she said, and buried her head in her hands, weeping. "I'm telling you the truth!"

Foster stood and walked back to Everton and Hiko; the deckhand looked openly skeptical, but Everton seemed almost . . .

Triumphant?

"Well?" Everton asked softly.

Foster sighed. "You're right, she's nuts. But *something* sure scared her. Let's get her to the bridge."

She turned back to the sobbing woman, scooping up a loose piece of electrical cord as she crouched down in front of her. She held out her other hand, trying to look as though she believed what Nadia had said; she didn't want to set her off again.

"Come on, I'll help you up."

Nadia let herself be pulled up, and Foster quickly looped the cable around her wrists, cinching it tightly.

The Russian realized the betrayal too late; she

started shrieking, clawing at Foster, but then Hiko was there to help and they dragged the screaming Nadia back up the stairs, Foster feeling very much like an asshole.

■ ■ ■

Woods held the totally weird little robot and a steadily growing coil of cable along with it as they followed the 'droid's connecting line down the dark corridor. Richie walked in front of him with a flashlight and the AK-whatever-it-was ready for action. Ahead of them somewhere was the faint sound of humming electricity, growing louder.

Woods was feeling no pain, but blurred flashes of disturbing thoughts and feelings kept coming up as they edged along. Steve Baker had told them to get down to Squeaky 'cause he wasn't there . . .

Woods frowned. Get to the *engine* room, to see what *happened* to little Squeaky. And Captain Everton had told them the same like a half hour ago, maybe longer. There had been blood, too. In the missile room by that one door.

He shook off the memories and picked up more cable, staying close to Richie. Richie was a good guy to be with after all, he knew about guns and high-tech stuff; they'd get to Squeaky once they figured out where the robot had come from—

Richie stopped suddenly and Woods looked up, reached for his own flashlight. The corridor had stopped in front of a door, and the sounds of working machinery were definitely coming from behind it.

Richie opened the door and hit at a light switch, but the room stayed dark, at least from what Woods could see. They both stepped inside, and Woods saw a shower of brilliant sparks, maybe twenty feet ahead in the humming room.

They both directed their lights at the source, and Woods felt his jaw drop.

No way.

They were in a workshop of some kind, lined with long tables and walls of tools. Thick cables seemed to hang from everywhere like jungle vines, looped across blinking computer consoles and dripping down from the shop tables. And connected to each swaying cable was a tiny, silvery robot, working efficiently away at building more tiny robots.

The beams of light glinted across slender metal legs and arms, each of the 'droids no more than a foot or so high. Some were vaguely humanoid in shape, arms and legs and flat, circuit-board bodies encased in metal. Others looked insectile, like the flying one that Woods still held—these skittered across the tables like mechanical spiders or crabs, multilegged and skeletal.

Woods stared at the creatures, amazed. It was like a series of miniature assembly lines, the robots passing small limbs back and forth, soldering and welding the pieces together, obvious to everything as they worked their separate tasks . . .

Richie reached behind and slapped at the power switch set next to the useless lights. All at once, every activity stopped; each robot seized, each tool died, leaving only silence and the smell of hot metal in the darkness.

Richie's walkie-talkie crackled suddenly and Steve's voice entered the room. He sounded tense.

"Richie, where are you guys?"

Richie snatched up the unit and spoke excitedly. "Steve! There's a machine shop down here with state-a'-the-art robotics that makes our stuff look medieval!"

The engineer wasn't interested. "Richie, I told you to get your ass down to the engine room! Are you deaf, are you brain-dead?"

Richie sighed. "We're comin', we're comin'—"

Suddenly the machines reactivated. All of them at once, and the small robots were back at work as though they'd never stopped.

Richie stuck his walkie back in his belt and hit the power switch again, toggling it back and forth. The 'droids continued their work, their cables swinging gently as they performed their production.

But they shouldn't have power anymore!

"Let's get out of here," Woods pleaded softly, but Richie ignored him, walking slowly towards one of the worktables. He seemed totally fascinated.

Woods shivered suddenly, violently. Someone was watching them; he could feel unseen eyes studying them from somewhere in the room.

He took a step toward Richie and his voice came out sharp, commanding. "Goddamn it, Richie, let's go!"

Richie held up one hand, watching a small robot that was soldering microcircuits. He reached down gently and poked at it.

The 'droid pivoted suddenly and held up one

strange arm, a device at one end that Woods had seen before; it was—

Thwap! Thwap!

Woods screamed as the nails buried themselves in his shoulder. He dropped everything, clutching at the horrible pain, and the 'droid fired again, the air suddenly alive with whizzing nails.

A second 'droid rotated, drove a whirling drill bit into the back of Richie's left arm. Richie howled, dove for one wall, and snatched up a fire ax from its mounts. He turned back to the table, screaming in fury as the drone with the nail gun continued to fire.

Woods scrambled across the dark room, trying to grab at his shoulder and unsling one of the automatic rifles at the same time. Richie brought the ax down again and again, chopping at the power cables that led to the table as nails clattered past him and ricocheted off metal.

There was sudden movement in the blackest shadows at the back of the room and Woods spun, saw a human figure dash out from one corner. There was a flash of bright fire and a loud popping—

He's firing at us!

Woods and Richie both hit the deck as the attacker sprayed the room with bullets, still running through the shadows at the rear of the shop. Woods raised his own weapon, saw Richie do the same, and they both leapt up, returning fire.

Together they backed out of the room, strafing the AKs across the tables, bullets peppering the walls, the robots, the cables, everything, in a deadly hail of explosive fire.

· 15 ·

Steve had found a shortcut through a scuttle on the C deck. The small passageway should take him straight to E, and he worked his way down the bolted ladder quickly, deeply worried about his partner. Hell, deeply worried about *everything*.

Squeaky, not answering. Richie and the helmsman off exploring somewhere, an insane Russian woman attacking them, sinking the tug—and the persistent feeling he'd had ever since they'd gotten the turbine going, one he couldn't seem to shake.

Someone's watching us from those goddamn cameras. Watching everything we say and do . . .

And twice since he'd left the others in sick bay, he'd heard noises—strange clicking noises and impressions of movement in the dark behind him. Both times he'd found nothing. The *Volkov* kept its secrets well, the ship veiled in silence and shadows ...

The walkie hissed static through the tight passage and Steve stopped, hoping desperately that Squeaky would be on the other end. He reached for the unit, his hope crushed as Richie shouted through the receiver.

"Steve, Woods is hurt! There's another Russian down here, he shot at us! Watch your ass!"

Christ, what next?

"Read you," he said. "How bad is Woods?"

He heard the helmsman in the background, his voice whiny and upset. "Tell him it's bad, Richie."

Richie continued. "He'll live, but he ain't in a good mood."

Steve tried to keep his voice controlled. "Get him to the engine room, we gotta get Squeak outta there."

"We're on our way," said Richie, and the walkie crackled to silence.

Steve continued down, overwhelmed with sudden anger at the deckhand's total inability to listen. How many times did Richie have to hear "Get to the engine room" before he'd bother paying attention?

Squeaky could be hurt, he could be trapped—

Steve didn't allow himself to follow the thought to its conclusion. His feet hit bottom; he was there.

He opened the watertight hatch at the base of the ladder, frowning. The lights were off. He clicked his flashlight on and pointed his shotgun out into the corridor, tracking with the beam of light across the hall. Nothing.

He realized that he was in the same corridor

as the engine room, that the scuttle had let out farther down the hall and opposite from where he and Squeaky had originally come down. He took a few steps out into the empty darkness and saw a panel of light set into the bulkhead, casting an elongated glow across the hall. It was the engine room.

Steve hurried to it, gave the corridor one last look before pressing his face to the door's observation window. Some of the lights were on, the engines were running, but his friend was nowhere in sight.

He hit the latch, but the door wouldn't budge. Steve frowned, backed up, and shone his light against the hatch; the job was smooth and professional. It had been welded shut.

He banged against the door, shouting. "Squeaky! *Squeaky!*"

No answer. Steve held his flashlight to the window, searching the corners for any sign of his partner. He saw Squeaky's walkie-talkie on a table, a crumpled pack of cigarettes next to it—

—*but where'd you go, man?* Squeaky wouldn't have left, not without his radio. And if he *had* spotted trouble and taken off, where was he now? And who had welded the door?

Someone was behind him. Steve wheeled around, dropping the flashlight as he jerked the shotgun up—

—and saw Richie step into the soft light, Woods next to him. Both men held AK-47s, and Steve saw that Woods had several more slung over one shoulder, as well as a stuffed munitions pack and—

—*a* grenade *launcher?*

Steve lowered the barrel, relieved to see them.

"Goddamn, you find their weapons locker?"

He stepped closer, saw that Woods had his left hand pressed against his right shoulder. Blood seeped between his fingers, and a wet stain radiated out from his wound, dripping down his arm.

"Shit, Woods, you're a mess. A Russian did this?"

Richie shook his head grimly. "No, a machine did that. With a nail gun."

Steve frowned, and Richie widened his eyes earnestly. "You're not gonna believe it till you see it, Steve! There's some really weird shit on this ship."

Steve reached for Woods's hand, trying to get a closer look, but Woods backed away. From the smell, he'd been drinking. A lot.

"He won't let you pull 'em out," said Richie.

"I need proper medical attention," said Woods. "Man, I ain't no fuckin' soldier, we shouldn't even *be* on this ship!"

Steve scowled. "Get a grip, Woods, you aren't dying."

He turned back to Richie, motioned at the hatch. "The engine room door's been welded shut. And Squeak ain't in there."

"Welded?" Richie reached for the latch, then examined the edges of the door. "You're right, man. Weird."

"What's happening here?" Steve asked softly, not really expecting an answer.

Woods frowned, sniffed the air. "Hey, you smell somethin'?"

Steve took a deep breath, ready to tell both men to straighten themselves up, stoned, drunk—and then he smelled it, too.

Decay, but combined with an odor of burnt meat. It was terrible, like roadkill on a hot day, cooked rotten meat—

—and something moved at the end of the dark corridor, something the size and shape of a man. Two yellowish green lights were set where a man's eyes should be, glowing out at them from the shadows.

Richie squinted. "Squeakman, that you?"

Steve gripped his shotgun tighter. "Squeaky?"

The lights moved closer.

Steve raised his voice, could hear fear in it as the moving figure shuffled forward, the rotten smell growing stronger. "Identify yourself!"

Richie and Woods sidled up beside him, and they all raised their weapons as the figure stepped into the soft light from the engine room, emerging from the gloom and into view.

"Holy shit . . ." Woods whispered.

It was alive, but it was only part human. The rest was metal and wire, cords and circuits set into flesh that was starting to decay. It was a man, half of his skull cleanly removed, the exposed brain glistening. Wires extended out from the gelatinous mass and twisted behind the creature. One hand held an acetylene torch, the other ended in a semiautomatic pistol, the grips of the Russian nine-millimeter melded somehow to bone and metal. Cracked, dripping flesh hung from the skeletal fingers.

The thing raised the pistol towards them, and as one, all three men opened fire.

■ ■ ■

Hiko stood with Foster and the captain on the bridge of the *Volkov,* all three of them casting uneasy glances at the crazy woman seated several feet away. Her hands were tied in front of her and she was eating a granola bar next to a table, her face angry and sorrowful at once as she stared blankly at the humming computers.

Hiko was unhappy with the whole situation. The wound in his leg was *mamae* and throbbed like a bastard, the others were still missing, and now Foster and Everton were arguing in heated whispers about what to do without addressing the real problem—that they were trapped on a strange and unfriendly ship in the middle of a typhoon.

Porangi, all of 'em. Nuts.

Foster was still trying to get Everton to consider their captive's repeated requests to shut the power down. "This ship belongs to the Russian government, Captain. And she's a senior officer."

"What the fuck was she hiding in a locker for?" Everton whispered angrily.

Hiko sighed. "Foster's got a point, Captain."

Nadia, the crazy, was watching them carefully. Everton walked a few steps farther away and they joined him, Hiko's leg aching miserably.

"Shut up, both of you," Everton hissed. "This ship was a derelict when we found her; her engines were down, her crew's either dead or deserted—she's up for grabs, and Olga Korbut over there knows it. Any admiralty judge in the world's gonna side with us—"

"You're all going to die," called Nadia, and Hiko scowled. Could she possibly shut up? He was sick of hearing about the horrible danger they were all in, sick and tired and angry.

Not as angry as Everton. "Hear that, Foster?

We're all going to die because *aliens* are on the ship. Officer or not, she's not mentally competent to run this vessel!"

Hiko sighed again. That was true, also.

Everton walked over to Nadia and towered over her, his cheeks flushed with high color. "I've got a man missing and I want some answers. And no 'Twilight Zone' shit this time."

Nadia stared up at him. "I can prove every word I said."

They locked gazes, and what Everton did next proved that he was, as *porangi* as she was. He unholstered his revolver suddenly and leveled it at her head.

"Bullshit. Five seconds, or I'm going to blow your head off. One . . ."

Foster shot a terrified look at Hiko and stepped forward, her voice high and anxious. "Wait! She was hiding in the sick bay, she doesn't know where Squeaky is."

Everton didn't look away from Nadia's cold and angry eyes. "Two . . . She knows. She dropped an anchor on my boat and *fired* on us. Three . . ."

Foster stepped closer, pleading now. "Put the gun down! Hiko—?"

Hiko shook his head slowly. He didn't want to see the woman die, but it wasn't up to him—and the pain in his leg was vicious. Besides, Everton was bluffing, he had to be. "Somebody dropped an anchor on me. I ain't feeling too sympathetic."

"Four . . ."

Everton pulled back the hammer and Nadia stared at him defiantly, steely cold. She was not afraid, and Hiko pushed away from the console he'd been leaning on and moved towards Everton, suddenly not sure if the captain was bluffing at all. The woman didn't *look* crazy in the face of *mate,* and that meant—Hiko didn't know what that meant.

"Goddamn it, Captain, *holster that gun!*" Foster cried.

Nadia only stared at Everton intensely, her voice cold. "Do it. Shoot me, I don't care. Just *shut the power off to this ship.*"

Foster grabbed the captain's arm, shoving the revolver away. "She's not going to tell you what you want to hear, Captain!"

"I'd like to hear what she has to say about this."

They all turned, saw Steve and Richie and Woods standing at the hatch, the three of them carrying a body. They walked onto the bridge, struggling beneath the weight of their load, a smell of rot drifting along with them.

They moved to the chart table where Nadia sat and slammed their stinking burden down. Hiko hobbled a step closer and felt every hair on his body stiffen and stand. He reached for his *wahaika* instinctively, clutching at it, but there was no comfort to be had, no respite from the nightmare laid out in front of them.

It seemed that the Russian wasn't crazy after all.

· 16 ·

Nadia looked away, wishing that the captain, Everton, had shot her.

It is too much! Oh, Alexi, how can I go on?

"What . . . the *fuck* . . . is that?" Everton, his expression stunned. He still held the revolver out but had apparently forgotten his promise to kill her.

One of the men who had carried the creature to the bridge spoke, the dark-skinned man. "Beats the hell outta us."

Nadia couldn't bear to look, not yet; she knew exactly what they saw. She studied the faces of the American crew, trying to fix names to each in an effort to subdue her breaking heart; these were the people who would live or die now, the men and woman who had yet to face the nightmare.

Everton, Foster, Hiko—and the young dark-haired man she'd seen before, he was Steve. The other two would be Woods and Richie, though she didn't know which from which. The pale blond man had been wounded in his shoulder; she decided that he must be Woods, because he seemed—weaker than the other, Richie. Richie was the one who had spoken so strongly over the radio.

They all wore the same face now as they stared at the horror in front of them; fascination and disgust played across their tired features in equal measure.

Nadia stood up slowly and looked down on the biomechanoid, trying to see it through her scientist's eyes—the tiny fiber optics that lay across the motor cortex, leading away to the partly exposed parietal lobe of the brain; the slivers of metal woven throughout the dermis and visible deep fascia, the tenosynovitis at the wrists—

She couldn't do it. "It is Alexi," she said softly. "My captain."

"This thing tried to *kill* us," said the wounded man; definitely Woods.

Hiko flared his nostrils, frowning. "Smells funky."

"Squeaky's missing and somebody's welded the engine room shut," said Steve.

Richie shot a dark glance at her and then addressed the others. "And *she's* got friends down there. Can somebody explain what the hell's going on?"

Everton finally lowered his revolver and she felt their eyes on her, all of them ready to listen now that they had seen.

Foster stepped closer to her, and Nadia saw

true regret on her face, an apology—and a will to survive in her serious gaze that was hauntingly familiar.

Only eight days ago, I was this woman . . .

"Finish your story," Foster said.

Nadia's bound hands were shaking. "I need a cigarette," she whispered.

Hiko handed Nadia's satchel to Foster, who rummaged through and pulled out her cigarettes and lighter. She handed one to Nadia, then lit it for her and stepped back.

Nadia inhaled deeply, blew out, and told them how it had happened.

■ ■ ■

"The thing that came onto this ship . . . *infested* the mainframe computer, the labs, the machine shops. It activated the halon fire extinguishers as we slept. Sixty-seven died, a quarter of the crew the first night."

The woman took another drag off her cigarette and Steve watched her, wanting to see the lie on her face, hear it in her voice—but her heavily accented English was brutally honest, her pale face betraying no hint of deceit.

"It cut us off from the machine shops . . . and started building. The little ones first, the gatherers."

Richie nodded. "Yeah, we saw a whole room full of them!" He glanced at Steve, still nodding. "That's what nailed Woods."

The woman went on, the smoke from her cigarette dismally reminding Steve of Squeaky. Just the thought of his partner, alone, somewhere on the *Volkov*—

"Then came something much more danger-ous." She glanced at the table, then looked away quickly as if it caused her pain.

"Made from parts of dead crewmen. Half man, half machine, a—biomechanism. Engineer-ing beyond our comprehension that can kill in horrible ways . . ." She took another deep drag.

"The crew quickly deserted, taking their chances in the sea. Only Alexi and I stayed to fight. We cut cables, destroying its ability to move through the ship—"

Foster interrupted gently. "What does cutting cables have to do with anything?"

"The machines are controlled by the—electri-cal energy in the computer. Cut off their source, their power . . . they die."

It finally hit Steve, all of the cables they'd seen—he reached for the frayed cord that led from the back of the biomechanoid and tapped at it thoughtfully.

Of course. But—what started it? How?

Woods had reached for his hip flask, fumbling out what looked like the last of the whiskey. Steve watched him upend the bottle with real envy; he suddenly wanted a drink very badly.

"So what *is* this thing?" Steve asked.

She took a last drag from her cigarette and dropped it to the deck, crushing it beneath one boot. "A life-form unlike anything we know. Ex-tremely intelligent. A life-form that is electrical in nature."

Richie frowned. "You mean—like lightning that can *think*?"

She nodded, reached up awkwardly to pull at a battered set of dog tags she wore. "And subject to the same laws of physics. It has no form, no shape; it's giving itself what it lacks, creating a new life-form using parts of the ship and crew. It's—evolving."

"Evolving into what?" Foster asked quietly.

The Russian didn't answer, and Steve could see it was because she didn't know; they all stared at one another, then back at the creature that she called Alexi, the bridge deathly silent—

—except for the droning hum of the computers that surrounded them, feeding themselves on the power that coursed through the vessel from the massive engine deep below.

■ ■ ■

Foster believed it, all of it. She had succeeded in rationalizing to herself each single event that had happened since they'd come aboard the *Volkov*, explaining to herself that it had been strange but not necessarily impossible; but the combination of her own intuition and the growing list of improbable events was too much to be denied when taken in full. Nadia's story explained everything—the missing crew, the anchor sinking the tug, the sense she'd had all along that they were being watched by something she couldn't name . . .

The—*creature* on the table in front of them only cinched it for Foster. Richie had taken out his penknife and was poking at the exposed brain tissue of the biomechanoid while the rest of them absorbed Nadia's story, each lost in their own thoughts. Nadia had closed her eyes, sat now with one trembling hand pressed lightly to her temple.

Foster leaned over to see what Richie was doing, swallowing dryly. There was a tiny circuit board implanted in the jellied mass; waveforms danced on a minute instrument screen connected to it by homonoid fibers. Richie was using his knife to peel back layers of the wet tissue, exposing wire threads and metal components like she'd never seen.

He continued probing, his expression one of stoned fascination. She watched as he followed a bundle of fiber optics down a metal-link spine, edging along with the tip of the blade.

"Look at this," he murmured, and Foster leaned in closer. "Right here is some kind of coil, a self-contained power supply built right into it . . ."

He looked up for a moment, saw that everyone was watching him. "This brain is still alive," he said softly.

Nadia turned to look, saw what he was doing, and winced. She stood up, moving opposite from Richie at the head of the table, a look of pain on her fragile features. Richie didn't even seem to notice, too involved in his morbid searching.

Nadia leaned down and whispered to the creature, her eyes bright with sorrow. "Alexi? Alexi—"

She went on in Russian, but the tone was clear; a mourning lament in her own language, each strange word a soft testament to her aching loss. Foster watched uncomfortably, wondering at the depth of emotion.

Her captain, but something more, too. Maybe—

Richie touched something and the creature's eyes snapped open, glowing yellow-green.

Foster reeled back instinctively, saw the shock and terror of the others as the biomechanoid focused on Nadia, one flesh and metal hand spasming, reaching up—

Nadia screamed as it clutched her arm. She lurched backwards, struggled to release herself, but the steel beneath the rotting fingers was solid, unyielding, and her hands were still tied.

Steve pulled his bowie knife and leapt forward, Hiko right behind with his strange club. Steve hacked at the arm of the creature, brutal chops that smacked wetly into the meat of the forearm and clanked against metal beneath the skin. Hiko beat at the circuitry lines that threaded the shoulder, crushing them against bone while Nadia continued to scream.

The thing's hand quivered and loosened, releasing its grasp. Nadia collapsed to the floor, sobbing as the biomechanoid fell back to the table, eyes open but unseeing.

Foster went to her, knelt down beside her as Steve and Hiko stepped away, turning to Richie.

"Leave the goddamn thing alone, Richie!" Steve gasped.

Richie sounded petulant, whiny. "I was just looking at it . . ."

"Touch that again and I will fucking kill you," Hiko breathed.

Nadia was shuddering, long strands of her blond hair sticking to her sweating, tearstained face.

"Are you all right?" Foster asked.

Nadia looked up at her, eyes wide and shocked. "It's Alexi. It's still Alexi," she said, then shook her head, denying her own words.

Foster rummaged through her pockets, came up with a handkerchief, and started to wipe at the woman's face—and froze as Everton broke his silence finally, erupting into a tirade of harsh words.

"This is bullshit, I've listened to this long enough! Aliens, my *ass;* this is something your government created, some medical experiment."

He stormed over to them, glaring down at Nadia. "Something went wrong, didn't it? Tell me the truth."

Nadia stared at him in anger and disbelief. "Alexi was no medical experiment, Alexi was my *husband.*"

Foster stood up quickly, astounded at Everton's blatant insensitivity and blindness. How could he deny what he must've known, what they all knew, deep down? The *Volkov* was wrong, it felt all wrong, far beyond any goddamn *experiment;* and there was a woman crying for the man she obviously loved right in front of him, her whole life shattered and—

"Could somebody *please* take a look at these nails in my shoulder?"

Foster stalked over to Woods, fuming. *Fuckin' whiny kiss-ass drunk helmsman, selfish bastards.*

She looked at Woods's bleeding shoulder, saw the nails protruding from his ripped shirt and the total self-pity in his drunken gaze. She reached forward with both hands and gripped the nails, checked the angle, and then yanked them out smoothly.

Woods howled and dropped to the floor as though she'd murdered him. She ignored him, moving to the window and holding up the nails, examining them. The light wasn't very good; she glanced out the window—

—and saw Leiah's churning eye wall, an immense tower of black water and raging wind about to slam into the hull of the ship.

· 17 ·

Oh shit . . ." Foster said weakly.

Richie looked up from the still flesh-machine on the table and suddenly day turned to night and the world tilted sideways.

Captain shouted, "Brace yourselves!"

He heard the crash of water against the *Volkov* as his feet suddenly lost the deck and he was thrown across the room backwards, along with everything on the bridge that wasn't bolted down. The lights dimmed and flickered, the shouts of the others lost to the violent, gusting rain that whipped through the broken windows.

Richie slammed into a console, his shoulder taking the brunt of the impact. He grabbed at the mounted frame, fingers scrabbling to get hold as the lights strobed—

—and the thing that had once been a Russian captain slid across the deck straight at him, the cold, stinking flesh of its heavy torso smacking up against his own. Richie opened his mouth to scream—and it started to move, a burst of digital code somewhere inside making the twisted limbs shudder and convulse.

Richie shrieked and somehow he was on his feet and halfway across the bridge even as the *Volkov* settled back into the heaving waves.

FUCKIN' FUCK—

He spun, terrified that it would be right behind him, but it still lay against the console, writhing horribly. It spasmed, flesh and fabric tearing together as the biomechanoid arched its back impossibly high—

—and a metal-meshed spine ripped through to the surface, bringing up bone, muscle, and human tissue woven with circuitry. Huge chunks of reeking body parts fell away, the creature pulling itself up and lurching across the deck in a spray of bloody fluids.

The thundering explosion of bullets suddenly overshadowed the howling storm and Richie hit the deck, covering his head with both arms. He turned his head, saw both Everton and Hiko firing their sidearms wildly at the staggering monster.

"What the fuck are you doing?" Steve shouted, and Richie turned his head the other way, saw that everyone else had gone down as ricochets pinged through the rocking bridge, chips of molded plastic and metal flying.

"Stop shooting! You're going to kill someone!" Foster screamed, and for once, Richie agreed with her; it was too close, someone was gonna get hit if they didn't listen.

Bits of the biomechanoid's tattered body were

spattering across the deck, the creature flailing its mangled arms as it collapsed next to Woods. Hiko and Everton stopped finally, and it flopped itself over, arching up to stare blindly into Woods's screaming face before it fell back to the deck. It quivered a moment, then lay still.

"We gotta get the fuck off this ship," said Richie, knowing that there was no way—and knowing just as surely that if he had to see anything like that ever again, he'd lose his fuckin' mind.

Another swell crashed against the *Volkov* broadside, tipping her into the foaming sea, and for one long, terrible second, Richie thought they would go over. Then she settled back, water spraying through the shattered glass as the typhoon screamed on.

He pulled himself upright, saw the others stumbling to their feet. Everton ran for the wheel, Foster to the flickering radar screen.

"Head her into the wind!" Steve yelled.

"Wind direction is east-northeast, velocity one-twenty!" Foster shouted.

Everton turned from the helm, the wheel spinning. "The controls are dead, she won't turn!"

"Captain, we take another hit like that and we'll roll!" Foster called.

Steve turned to Everton, still shouting to be heard over the storm. "We can manually steer her from the engine room, we can run the ship from there!"

Everton stared at him, confused. "You said the door's welded shut!"

"We'll *cut* the fuckin' door!"

The captain barely hesitated. "All right." He motioned at the Russian, adding, "Bring her!

And keep her tied up till we sort this out!"

Richie grabbed up his AK-47 and turned to Woods, the helmsman still sitting on the deck, seemingly paralyzed by the lifeless creature that sprawled a few feet away. Richie picked up the munitions pack and the RPG, slinging them over his shoulder.

"Get off your ass, Woods," Richie growled, suddenly furious at the man for being so frightened—and although it hurt to admit, because deep down, he felt the same way. They were going back into an environment capable of producing mechanical zombies, of shaping electricity into abominations that would try to steal their bodies . . .

Not me, Richie decided, and felt every fiber of his being sing agreement; he'd blow up the whole goddamn ship before they took him down.

■ ■ ■

They all moved down the stairwell in a tense group, Richie and Baker in the lead, the two women and Hiko behind them, then Everton and Woods. All of them had their weapons drawn and pointed up, careful to take into account the sudden shifts of the rocking vessel.

Everton noticed that the Russian was having trouble keeping her balance with her wrists bound; petty as it was, he felt a certain satisfaction each time she stumbled. The woman was a menace and a liar; she'd spun up a fantastic tale to terrify his crew and had already tried to kill them once—not to mention violently assaulting him like some kind of common criminal. Her minor discomfort didn't begin to make up for it, but it certainly made *him* feel better.

They had reached the hatch to C deck. Baker and Richie stepped out into the dark corridor with their flashlights while the rest of them waited nervously. Woods in particular was breathing like a fish out of water, although he'd finally stopped bleeding. Everton felt sorry for him; of all the crew, he was the only one who seemed to remember who the captain was.

The two crewmen walked back in, looking frazzled and anxious.

"All clear?" Everton asked.

"Clear," said Baker.

"Clear." Richie nodded easily, but his eyes darted back and forth and he'd developed a tic at one side of his mouth.

Everton nodded, and they moved cautiously into the corridor, Richie and Baker leading the way. The stairs were staggered at this end of the ship; Richie had said they'd find the next well only a few hundred feet past where they'd been let out—

Foster stopped suddenly and Everton almost ran into her. He felt a rush of irritation—and then realized that the boat wasn't heaving as violently as it had been before.

"The ship's turning," she said, and reached into her pocket, pulling out a compass.

"We've altered course," said Everton. *Damn it!*

Foster studied the compass under Baker's light, then looked up at Everton, apprehensive. "We just turned twenty degrees into the wind. This ship is steering itself."

Nadia shook her head. "Ships don't steer themselves . . ."

Well no shit, *Natasha.*

Everton glared at her. "You're right. So who is? One of your Russian friends?"

The woman looked at him coldly. "I told you. They're all dead."

He barely resisted an urge to slap her; apparently she didn't realize that she was *their* hostage, that she was no longer in control—

—*communist bitch, out here performing immoral, insane atrocities on human beings and then acting like* I'm *the bad guy.*

It wasn't all that surprising that she would continue to lie. She had to know that she would be crucified for all that she'd done once they made it back to land, her and her team of scientists. Questioning her about what her comrades were planning was pointless; he just hoped they'd be able to use her to get to the others. They were mad, all of them—and as soon as he collected his salvage fee, he'd see to it that she got what was coming to her.

"There's a staircase leading down," said Richie, motioning to a hatch farther along.

"One more deck," said Steve.

They moved as a tight group towards the stairwell, through the silence of the shifting darkness. Everton saw a security door in the flashes of light, complete with a fingerprint keypad; the Russians were a shifty lot, and he felt an almost overwhelming impatience to get to the engine room. They could be taking the ship to a Russian port or deliberately sabotaging it to keep the truth from getting out. Even though the *Volkov* had been turned in to the wind, their need to take control was no less urgent; the ship *belonged* to them now, it was theirs and—

BAM! BAM! BAM!

Everyone froze, but the pounding against the bulkhead farther down the corridor continued, the sounds resonating loudly through the empty hall.

Someone was behind one of the hatches, and he wanted out.

■ ■ ■

Steve turned back the way they'd come, his surprise quickly turning to hope. The urgent sound was close, maybe halfway down the corridor past the stairs.

"Shit, what's that?" Woods was terrified, his voice cracking.

Steve wanted to laugh out loud. "Could be Squeak! C'mon!"

Woods shook his pale, sweating face vehemently. "Uh-uh, I'm not goin' that way. It could be *anything* swingin' loose—"

"I *said*, it could be Squeaky."

He looked at Everton, but the captain was apparently not going to argue with him. Steve walked through the group, actually feeling their combined tension like an electrical charge. He was scared, too—who wouldn't be after seeing that *thing* walking around?—but if it was his partner . . .

Hang on, Squeak!

He took the lead and Richie fell in next to him, his knuckles white against the automatic rifle. Steve forced himself to walk slowly as the insistent pounding filled his ears; had he been alone, he would have run for the hatch—but there was no way the others were up for it. Woods was a wreck, Everton was acting increasingly weird—even Richie seemed pretty tight; he'd bought in to Nadia's story all the way, as had Foster. Steve wasn't planning on voting till he had more information . . .

They edged forward, the *Volkov* rumbling around them from the storming seas outside. The pounding was coming from a closed hatch up ahead, a small window inset at eye level. As they reached the door, the banging suddenly stopped.

Hiko shone his light through the window and Steve grinned, felt a huge weight lift off of him; he *knew* it!

"It *is* Squeaky," Hiko said, and the pounding started again as he reached for the latch.

Richie suddenly shouted from behind him, startling them all.

"Don't open it! Don't fuckin' open it!" His voice cracked in fear, his eyes wide and rolling.

Hiko hesitated, and Steve shook his head, amazed and disgusted. Jesus, were they *blind*? Richie had smoked too much weed, gotten paranoid. He pushed Hiko roughly out of the way.

"Move over," he growled, and threw the latch, so relieved that he almost wanted to cry. He'd been fighting to keep his hopes up, but it had been getting harder, eating him up inside. Everything was different now.

He backed up a step and Squeaky walked out into the corridor, expressionless—and for just a second, Steve felt a cold uncertainty grip him. Why wasn't he smiling?

He swallowed and backed up another step, the group behind him.

"Squeaky?" Steve's voice was a whisper.

Squeaky looked at him. "Steve."

Squeaky's voice was as blank and unreadable as his face.

Steve's grin faded, and the coldness crept back. "What's wrong with you?"

His partner took another step forward. "Nothing. Now."

Steve saw it then, and felt his mind threaten to rip apart from the horrible wash of emotions that crashed down over him.

Cables ran down Squeaky's back and off into the dark of the opened hatch. And in the shadows behind him, something else moved.

· 18 ·

Foster stared in horror at the creature that stood in front of them, swaying gently with the motion of the ship. It looked like the engineer, spoke with his voice—but the glassy eyes no longer sparkled with humor or intelligence; the muscles of his—of *its* face were slack, rendering it characterless, devoid of personality. He wasn't Squeaky, not anymore.

Her shocked gaze traveled to the tall, shadowy figure behind Squeaky—and froze there. What she saw was so impossible that she couldn't fit her mind around it, couldn't accept what her eyes were telling her.

Can't be, no way, doesn't exist—

Steve's face was pale and waxy. "What the *fuck* is that?"

"Something *I've* never seen before," Nadia whispered.

The monstrosity was at least seven feet tall, squatting in the darkness like a praying mantis, its four legs a grotesque amalgamation of flesh and metal. Where the head should have been were what appeared to be two human brains, encased in a thick, gelid goo, video lenses and probing beams of light underneath. Foster counted three, four arms, two of them mechanical, two of them torn and tattered and definitely human.

The creature took a strange, sliding step past the Squeaky-thing and ripped through the thick hatch, the squeal of tortured metal finally breaking their stunned immobility.

As one, they raised their weapons and opened fire, backing away as the explosive rounds smacked into tissue and ricocheted off metal. Chunks of flesh were torn from the terrible creature, spattering against the bulkhead as it advanced like a mutant spider, seemingly unharmed by the rain of bullets.

Jesus, what is *it*—

Everton suddenly pushed through them, shoving between Hiko and Richie to get away from the oncoming creature. His panicked gaze was unseeing, his face sweating and flushed. Foster only narrowly missed shooting him as he stumbled past her and collided with Hiko, almost knocking him down.

Like a chain reaction, Woods tripped against Hiko and fell heavily to the floor, the sound lost in the deafening clatter of gunfire. He scrambled backwards, clawing and kicking at the bolted deck to get away, an expression of insane terror on his pallid face.

The creature that had been Squeaky lunged forward, impossibly fast, snatching Woods up as

if he weighed nothing and lifting him into the
air. The seven foot monster spidered forward
and in a single, brutal movement, plunged its
mechanical arms into Woods's flailing body,
puncturing his chest and belly with one powerful
thrust. *"Woods!"* Everton screamed, but Woods
was beyond hearing, his body spasming violently
as blood poured from the gaping wounds, gush-
ing down the Squeaky-thing's arms. Squeaky
tossed the broken body effortlessly across the
corridor and it slammed into the wall with a sickening wet *smack*, bones snapping as it fell in a
bloody, crumpled heap.

The biomechanoid Squeaky turned—

—and looked directly into the barrel of
Steve's shotgun. Steve was trembling, his finger
against the trigger. He looked feverish, sick with
emotions that Foster couldn't begin to name as
the thing that had been Squeaky cocked its head,
staring at him.

Steve lowered the gun and backed away.

As soon as he was clear, the rest of them
opened fire again. The biomechanisms advanced
towards them, impervious to the thundering
rounds that tore into them, leaving smoking
black holes in metal threaded tissue.

The group backed up the corridor, still firing.

Nadia turned and ran. Foster shot a look back,
saw that she was at a security hatch not far away,
her tied hands raised to the keypad.

Whatever you're doing, hurry!

The biomechanoid showed no sign of stopping. Squeaky's upper body was riddled with
seeping wounds, flaps of skin torn from his face
and neck, and still it walked forward, arms raised
as if to express fellowship. That was somehow

the worst of all—that it looked like Squeaky with his hands held up in supplication as they mercilessly blasted away at him.

Nadia was shouting over the deafening gunfire, standing at the door that she'd opened. Everton was the first there, followed by Richie and Hiko, both of them still firing. Steve waited for Foster to back to the door, then hustled both her and Nadia through the hatch before piling in behind them.

Steve pushed the vaultlike door shut and slammed down the manual latch. He fell against it, breathing heavily, his eyes wide and glassy with shock.

Foster went to him immediately, realizing that however awful it had been for them, it had been worse for Steve; Woods was dead, killed by a thing that had been Steve's partner and closest friend.

"That wasn't Squeaky, Steve," she said softly. "I don't know what that was, but it wasn't him."

Steve closed his eyes and Foster looked away, wondering how long it would be before Squeaky or his aberrant sidekick came knocking at the door—and how long they could hold out against any creature that bullets couldn't kill.

■ ■ ■

Nadia studied what the intelligence had done to the communications room, filled with an exhausted nostalgia for that last morning. It seemed like years had passed since she'd sat here, gloating over her chess game with Lonya. She'd been surrounded by her peers, doing her work in a safe and sane world that she understood—before the last transmission from MIR had come and taken it all away.

Some of the lights were on, exposing remnants of that terrible morning. The radio equipment was smashed, but many of the computer screens were still intact; they flashed now with biological diagrams and electrical schematics that were alien even to her. She could see the burn scars on the consoles, the stains of blood on the floor. Alexi had been drinking his Earl Grey, sitting where Everton now sat . . .

She realized that Captain Everton was staring at her with an expression of pure malice—but she could see also that he finally believed.

Wonderful. He is convinced, now that the proof of it has killed another of his crew—and he acts as if the fault is mine. What's wrong with him?

Hiko limped to one of the workstations and frowned over at her. "Where are we?"

"Communications room," she said.

Richie wheeled around excitedly. "The communications room, we can call for help!"

He went to the crushed console of the transmitters, picking up a handful of ripped circuitry and looking up, surprised.

"This is trashed. Who did this?"

"I did," said Nadia tiredly.

He scowled at her. "The radios on the bridge were trashed—did you do that, too?"

Nadia realized that they hadn't had time to consider everything, to understand the nature of the intelligence; in spite of her impatience, she kept her voice low and controlled.

"I destroyed every transmitter on this ship; if it transmitted on, it can surely transmit off. To another ship, an island . . . anywhere."

Richie ignored her, began prodding the ripped circuitry, and she looked at the others, wondering if they fully understood what she was telling them. Everton had stood and was pacing, his jaw clenched, his mind elsewhere; Hiko watched data scroll across the monitor screens. Steve still leaned against the thick door, staring off into space—only Foster was watching her, the woman's mouth set in a thin line as she nodded slowly.

She is perhaps the smartest of them, that one; she's afraid, but she listens—

There was a burst of static and Nadia's heart plummeted into her gut. She whipped around, saw Richie with his personal radio unit out and open, wires hooked to the circuitry of the transmitter board.

"You didn't smash this—Mayday, Mayday!"

"No, don't!" Nadia cried, struggling to her feet—

—and a burst of gunfire exploded through the room, the transmitter blown into smoking pieces.

"Damn, what the hell—" Richie started, and they all turned, shocked—and saw Everton standing there, his pistol drawn, a desperate, triumphant grin on his hateful face.

" 'Fraid I can't let you do that, Richie," he said.

Nadia was surprised, didn't think he'd been listening to her; perhaps he wasn't as ignorant as she'd thought.

"Captain, are you out of your fucking *mind*?" Richie asked, incredulous.

Everton's gaze darted around the room wildly. "I'm not going to let another ship salvage this vessel!"

They all stared at him, a long moment of silence heavy with dawning comprehension. Nadia understood finally, why he'd been so willfully obstinate, so set against allowing that she might be telling the truth.

He means to claim this ship as derelict! And he can't do that if there is anyone aboard. Anyone sane *aboard . . .*

Foster was closest to the captain, and as the rest of them sat or stood in the room, still digesting the pointless, greedy motivation of their leader—

—Foster swung, smacking Everton square on the jaw. He was knocked down by the force of her blow, his revolver skipping across the floor.

"You're no longer in charge," she said coldly.

Everton looked up pleadingly at the other men, one hand pressed to his face. "You going to let her get away with that?"

They stared back at him in silence, and Nadia felt a shaking relief as she studied their grim faces, saw the anger in their weary gazes. He was fighting for money; they were fighting for their lives.

Foster turned away, came to her, and quickly untied the wrapped wire that encircled her wrists. Nadia blew out slowly, rubbing at the marks. Perhaps they had a chance now; they knew what they were up against and Everton would be ignored—

BANG!

Nadia jumped up, startled. A heavy shelf next to the hatch went over, crashed to the floor as a huge impact outside shook the entire room. A dent had appeared in the thick metal of the security door.

The intelligence wanted them. And judging from the incredible force of its single blow, they had very little time before it succeeded.

■ ■ ■

Hiko spun around, grabbed a loose table next to the fallen shelf, and rammed it against the door. Steve ran to a console and ripped out a length of wire, then hurried to the hatch and tied the handle down.

BANG! BANG! BANG!

Three more gigantic welts appeared in the metal, and Hiko pushed frantically against the table, knowing that it was useless in the face of such power. He did it anyway, just as Steve had tied the latch; they had to do *something*.

"How many of these things are there?" Steve shouted over another hammering strike.

"What do they want from us?" Hiko cried. The creatures were relentless, pounding, and he was terrified that they would break through soon.

"Why don't we ask it!" Richie called, and Hiko looked away from the welted metal, back at the frightened faces of the others.

"What are you talking about?" Foster shouted.

Hiko understood suddenly, just as it dawned on Steve.

"Richie's right!" Steve shouted. "Let's just *ask* it!"

The Russian *wahine* was nodding, and Richie ran to one of the computers and sat down, snatching at the keyboard. He looked down at it, scowling, then at the board next to it. He quickly disconnected the first and plugged in the other.

Steve jerked his head at a heavy-looking desk a few feet away, and Hiko nodded. They hurried over and grabbed the edges, grunting, half carrying it to block the hatch, Hiko kicking the small table away with his uninjured leg.

It was the best they could do. The two of them crowded around where Richie sat, frowning at the foreign language that crawled up the screen in front of him.

Nadia leaned over him and tapped quickly at the keys, calling up a language window. She scrolled to English and clicked, Richie shooting her a look of thanks. Outside, the mighty pounding continued.

Richie typed quickly, his dark fingers flying over the keys.

Who are you?

The sentence hung there at the top of the green-glowing screen, and suddenly a list of numbers and icons whipped across the monitor beneath it, rows of ones and zeros. Hiko recognized it as binary code; his sister was a *kaiwhakamahi rorohiko;* she programmed this stuff for a living.

The code stopped flashing suddenly and the computer brought up an English dictionary file, began flipping through the information at incredible speed. The computer found the words, stopped on *who,* then *are,* then *you.* A definition appeared beside each—

—and the banging at the hatch suddenly stopped.

·19·

They all froze in the sudden silence of the communications room, tensing for whatever came next. Steve realized that he was somehow more afraid than he had been when the—*thing* in the hall had started pounding. They'd made contact with the creature, the alien that had destroyed Squeaky and murdered Woods and God knew how many others—

A horrible, high-pitched shriek emitted from the computer's speaker, followed by an even more terrible voice—low and inflectionless but malevolent all the same. As it spoke, the words appeared on the monitor beneath Richie's typed question.

I AM AWARE.

Steve looked at Hiko, Foster, at Nadia—even Everton, who stood several feet away and stared at them, stricken. The thing was communicating with them—what did they ask it, what *should* they ask it?

Foster slid next to Richie in front of the console, chewing at her lower lip. She reached over and tapped at the keys.

We mean you no harm.

Steve nodded; he sure as hell *felt* a lot of "harm," but this could be their only chance— make it understand that they didn't want to fight . . .

. . . *before it does to us what it did to Squeak.*

The computer spun through more files. This time the words were silent, appearing only on the screen.

LIFE-FORM ANALYSIS COMPLETE. SPECIES IS DESTRUCTIVE, INVASIVE, NOXIOUS. HARMFUL TO THE BODY OF THE WHOLE.

Richie typed, *What species?*

MAN.

The files started flipping through definitions again, as if searching for exactly the right words to finish its message. It finally stopped, blinking on the definition for *virus.*

YOU ARE VIRUS.

"Great, that's just great," Richie mumbled. "It thinks we're germs." He hesitated a moment, then typed, *What do you want from us?*

The computer searched, and the answer appeared in the form of a list. Steve frowned, confused by the message.

- *VISCOUS NEUROLOGICAL TRANS-MITTERS*
- *OXYGENATED TISSUES*

- *APONEURUS SUPERIORUS PAPEL-
  BRAI*

He read aloud the final line, stumbling over the pronunciation. "Aponeurus Superiorus Papel—?"

Nadia spoke softly, not looking away from the screen. "It's part of the optic nerve."

Richie looked up at him, his eyes rolling in panic. "Spare parts—it wants us for *spare parts*."

Steve looked back at the computer monitor, feeling a dread too deep for words. It didn't just want to kill them; it wanted to *dissect* them . . .

COMMUNICATION TERMINATED.

The screen went dead, and immediately the pounding at the hatch began again.

■ ■ ■

Richie stood up and grabbed his AK-47, reassured by the weight of it. His heart was hammering against his ribs like a scared rabbit in a cage, had been since that fuckin' nightmare had gotten Woods. He felt trapped, each thundering blow to the hatch sending the alien's *real* message loud and clear. They were gonna die, all of them.

Nadia raised her voice to be heard over the banging at the door. "It must be destroyed."

"How?" Foster asked.

Hiko looked at Nadia, talking fast and frightened. "You said this thing is electrical—like lightning. What happens when lightning hits water? It grounds out, it dies. So we could kill this thing!"

Richie shook his head. "Yeah, but we'd have to sink the ship to do that—"

—and maybe that's the way it ought to be; you wanna end up like Squeakman, some fuckin' alien slave?

"You said this thing is in the computer, right?" Foster asked. "Where's the mainframe?"

The banging was getting louder, more insistent. They were standing here talking about computers when there was a *monster* on the other side of the bulkhead, created by a thing that wanted to, to—

"D deck, below us. But it'll be well protected," said Nadia.

"We gotta get to that computer," said Steve. "But first we have to find a way out."

Richie backed away from them, scooping up the rocket and the pack as he separated himself from them in the pounding thunder. They were dead already, he was standing in a room with dead people; they just didn't have the sense to lie down.

Not me, NOT ME!

"I'll show you a way out," he said, and before he could say any more, the bulkhead next to the metal hatch tore open with a rending screech.

Human arms pushed through the ruptured steel, widening the hole. A face pocked with bullet holes forced its way through, the jagged metal of the torn opening peeling back farther under Squeaky's enhanced grip. Great flaps of fabric and skin were shredded from the shoulders of the engineer as he clawed and wriggled to get through. Squeaky didn't look much like Squeaky anymore.

Richie leveled the AK-47 at the head of the struggling abortion and let loose.

Round after round chopped into its head and

back, obliterating the features of the monster, stopping it. Flesh tore away from bone, revealing bits of glittering metal and wire patterned underneath.

"Steve."

The stammering thing backed out as Richie emptied the clip, the last few bullets hitting the wall across the dark corridor.

The AKM fell silent and it was gone—at least for now. Richie edged away, swapping the automatic rifle for the grenade launcher and turning around when he was a safe distance from the gaping, bloodstained hole.

He faced the others, saw the expressions of fear and shock, the anguish in Steve's dark eyes.

No, you're dead already, all of you, just like Squeaky, and you'll be coming for me *then.*

"You people do what you want," he said, and pumped the launcher easily. "I got my own plan."

He turned, faced the back wall, and stepped away from the bulkhead, sighting through the optical above the tube and placing the mount against his shoulder.

KABOOM!

Fire shot out of the back through the conical blast shield, and when the smoke cleared, a four-foot hole had opened up at the back of the room; the armor-piercing capacity of the 58.3-millimeter grenades was fucking *massive,* and firepower was the only chance he had. Fuck these people and their fuckin' sabotage and their schemes and their fear; he was safer on his own.

Another corridor was revealed beyond the blackened rupture of steel. Richie moved to the new exit, talking to the victims in the room as he strode forward.

"Spare parts, my *ass,* that's not gonna happen to me—that's *not* gonna happen to me! I'm outta here!"

He stepped through the hole, away from the walking dead and into a destiny that he was going to control.

■ ■ ■

"Richie's gone postal, man," Hiko blurted out.

It would have been funny if the situation weren't so monumentally horrible. Foster felt sick, unable to believe what they'd just witnessed. Things were happening too fast. Woods, Squeaky—the alien being, telling them what it would do if it got hold of them . . .

All in less than two hours. It sank the tug, got to Squeaky, killed Woods—and now Richie, cracking under the strain. Already feels like we've been here forever, but we boarded this thing less than two hours ago.

Steve walked to the blasted hole that the grenade had created and leaned out cautiously into the dim corridor, searching. He looked back at them and nodded once.

"At least he found a way out," said Foster. "Let's go."

She picked up her flashlight and an automatic rifle that Richie had left behind, handing it to Nadia. Steve or Hiko would still have clips for the .32, Steve had his shotgun.

It's the best we can do. Not enough, but it's all we have.

Steve stepped into the corridor, Hiko and Nadia behind him. Foster turned and saw Everton just standing there, staring.

"Are you coming?"

The captain didn't answer for a moment. His eyes were bright with absolute hatred, and when he finally spoke, his words dripped spite.

"Do what you want. You're all going to get yourselves killed."

Foster found suddenly that she didn't give a shit *what* he thought; their captain had exercised consistently crappy judgment all the way, had made it perfectly clear again and again that his narcissism was too deeply ingrained for him to lead them effectively. If he wanted to go it alone, to die alone, that was his decision—too bad, but she wasn't going to waste her breath trying to talk him out of it. She turned and exited without another word.

The corridor was narrow but empty, no movement except for the rocking sway of the deck beneath them and the flicker of lights overhead. Nadia pointed to the partly opened hatch at the end of the corridor; stairs, going down.

They hurried to the hatch, Steve leading the way, Hiko limping beside Nadia, Foster bringing up the rear. She kept herself half turned, sidling along in hopping steps to watch their backs. As they reached the stairs, Hiko spoke up.

"So who *is* in charge?"

Steve stopped, turned his dark gaze towards her, and raised an eyebrow. She looked back at him, not sure what to say.

It didn't matter anymore, not at this point. They would live or they would die, and passing on the title of "leader" wasn't going to change the outcome either way.

Steve apparently felt the same. He moved to Hiko's side, supporting the hobbled man, and together they headed down the stairs to whatever waited for them below.

· 20 ·

Everton rubbed at his jaw absently, not sure what to do. He sank down into a bolted chair, staring blankly at the gaping hole that his mutinous crew had left by.

He'd been so sure that the Russian had been lying, and who could blame him? An alien from the MIR, an entire crew throwing themselves at the mercy of a typhoon—anyone with half a brain in their head would call it bullshit. The creature that Baker and the other two had brought up to the bridge was amazing, true, but a team of scientists could have created something like that, what with medical technology being what it was these days; a Russian prisoner, experimented on by doctors as some kind of weapon, perhaps . . .

Seeing Squeaky had changed everything. There simply hadn't been enough time to—to *alter* a man like that, no matter how sophisticated the process. It had killed Woods, the only crewman worth anything to him, and yes, he'd been afraid—but he was willing to admit that, and would have admitted that he'd been wrong, too, had anyone bothered to ask. It was nothing to be ashamed of, people make errors in judgment—but had they troubled themselves to see *his* side of things? Had they remembered that there was a lot to be considered, decisions to be weighed carefully before running off half-cocked? No. No, of course not.

And what do I get for trying to protect my interests, to look after our *futures? I get decked by an uppity bitch who thinks she knows better than me—and deserted by the rest of them, my loyal "crew"* . . .

He supposed that he shouldn't have expected any better; times had changed, all sense of duty or honor lost to people like Baker and Foster. When Everton had first started out, he wouldn't have *dared* to treat his captain so disgracefully, nor would his shipmates; disregarding an order would have earned any one of them a serious beating, and rightfully so. Discipline was a thing of the past, it seemed. The worst mistake he'd made had been to trust his own crew to do their jobs and follow orders—and he sincerely hoped that they all would live long enough to regret their betrayal.

He sighed, looking around the empty room aimlessly. It was pointless to curse them or his own rotten luck; the question now was how would *he* survive? The others didn't stand a chance, which meant it was up to him to figure out a way to destroy the creature . . . except he

had a single .455 and a mere handful of rounds—
two speed loaders, ten bullets. The aberration
that had been Squeaky had taken ten times that
and was probably still running around . . .

*I don't stand much of a chance, either. If only
there were a way to talk to the creature, make it
see—*

Everton's gaze settled on the computers that
the others had used to contact it. The alien had
turned them off when it was finished talking to
Richie and Foster—but it hadn't talked to *him*
yet, had it?

He walked to the silent machines, frowning
thoughtfully. Assuming he could get through to
it, what would he say? What *could* he say to get
himself out of this with his skin intact?

*That's the wrong question—what I should be
asking myself is what does the* it *want that I can
provide, what would make* me *valuable to the
creature?*

"You want to talk to me?"

Everton smiled suddenly, sat down in front of
the keyboard, and looked up at the surveillance
camera, waiting. A second later, the screen
blinked to soft green life.

He kept his message brief and to the point,
pecking at the keys slowly with his index fingers.
The computer searched as he wrote.

Everton is the dominant life-form.

I am Everton.

*I will help you bring this ship to port. New Zea-
land, Australia, anywhere you want.*

He waited, wiped nervously at his upper lip
with the back of one hand. It wasn't like he owed
them anything, was it? If Foster or Baker or any
one of them had been smarter, they'd have

thought of it first; instead, they'd decided every man for himself, *they'd* set up the rules here. And it wasn't like there was any other choice . . .

. . . *and they'll be sorry when they realize what a monumental error they've made, treating me this way—*

Letters flashed across the screen. Everton frowned, squinting at the message.

E DECK, WORKROOM 14.

There was a clicking noise behind him. He spun around, heart pounding—and realized that it was the magnetic lock of the security hatch. The creature had unsealed it for him.

Everton stared at the door for a long moment, thinking about what this meant, what it *could* mean. Finally, he started to grin.

If he worked this right, he could end up a very wealthy man.

■ ■ ■

Richie sat on the floor of the dark missile room, carefully unscrewing the nose cap of the Russian grumble, his AK-47 close at hand. Technically the missile was a SAM-6, or at least he was pretty sure; it had been a while since he'd had to know specs and titles. All these things had their own little names, grunt, grumble. Range of around eighty klicks, this one, basic SAM with a flight speed somewhere about Mach three. Of course, it didn't matter what it was called; the fuse, the triggering mechanism beneath the cap, was still gonna be the ticket to insuring the success of his operation.

The closest he'd ever come to combat had been back in 1975, straight out of AIT when the

Seventh had been running refugee evacs from
Cambodia and South Vietnam—and he hadn't
seen a single attack. But he felt like he understood the combat experience now in a way that
he'd only heard about before. It was like he'd
been asleep his entire life and suddenly woke up;
his senses had sharpened, his thinking brain had
been overthrown by an animal instinct that
sought only to keep him alive. It was exhilarat-
ing, and he'd felt his fears and anxieties falling
away with each step he'd taken away from the
sheep back in the communications room. Their
tensions had been jamming his frequencies and
he hadn't even realized it until he'd gotten away
from them.

He didn't really *know* any of those people, but
he knew enough not to trust them with his survival. Hiko was a follower, no capacity for indi-
vidual initiative; Everton had lost his fuckin'
mind, had shot at the radio a foot in front of his
face with no thought for Richie's life. Baker
might've been okay, but Foster and the Russian
had him thinkin' like a civilian . . .

Can't think like that, gonna get yourself offed
in this place. Probably dead already listenin' to
those women, worrying about pullin' plugs.

"I know what's goin' on," he mumbled, com-
forted by the sound of his sure voice in the still
room. He sounded confident; he sounded like a
man with a plan.

"They ain't gettin' me, my brain's not becoming a hard drive for some biomechanoid alien
fuck—"

There was something behind him, somewhere
in the room.

Richie froze. He didn't breathe, didn't twitch—

even his heart held still as he listened to the darkness, feeling for the sound, the disruption of space—

A scratching on the floor.

Richie whipped around, the rifle up and firing before it could move. The bullets struck metal, sent something skittering backwards with a shrill steel screech. There was a drift of burnt circuitry—then silence.

He picked up the flashlight and looked. A 'droid, like the ones in that workshop. This one was crablike, a low, flat body with multiple legs. A long, thin cord trailed off through the battered hatch that Woods had found earlier, but he'd blown enough holes in it to kill it. There was a tangle of wire extending from the robot's shattered belly, embedded with small, triangular metal pieces.

He reached over and yanked one of the components from the wire, holding it up in the beam of light.

"I could use this, this is a good part," he said, nodding.

He went back to carefully unscrewing the cap of the grumble, still nodding. Nice of the alien to send down a few extra parts; if it wasn't gonna phone home, it might as well make itself useful.

Richie stopped thinking, went back to simply being aware, feeling and being. He had a lot of work to do.

■ ■ ■

With each cautious step they took away from the stairwell, Nadia felt her fear grow. Steve walked with her, shining his flashlight down the first corridor and then the intersecting passage as she led them towards the main computer room on D. It was dark and silent except for the occasional rumble of the crashing seas outside and their own breathing, harsh and frightened in the stillness.

Where are they? The intelligence should have all of its creatures here, guarding its home.

That they had not been attacked already scared her more than anything; what weapon did the intelligence have, that it could afford to let them get this far? She could see the confusion on Steve's face, see it on Foster's each time she looked back; Hiko was concentrating too hard on walking for her to tell if he'd noticed . . .

She stopped at the turn to the next hall, then motioned towards a bulkhead hatch to the next corridor, what she'd always thought of as the Cold Hall; the temperature in the computer room was kept low. Now it felt the same as every other on the ship—strange and ominous, threatening, the air dead and still.

They all nodded and she led the way, gripping the Kalishnikov tightly. Her loose hair swung across her face, and she wished she'd thought to tie it back before they'd come down. She wouldn't even risk brushing at it now, too afraid to take her fingers from the automatic weapon.

Nadia tilted her head at a closed door midway down the corridor, illuminated by Steve's light.

"That door down there leads to the main computer room," she whispered.

They moved in a tight group through the Cold Hall, Hiko leaning against Foster, Steve's flashlight flickering through the darkness in shaking arcs. When they reached the door, they huddled

there for a moment. Nadia felt adrenaline coursing through her veins, sweat matting the hair to
her skull as she checked her rifle yet again.

"I thought you said this would be well protected," whispered Steve.

Nadia shook her head. There was no explanation—

*—except that it has the means to stop us inside
the room before we can touch it. Instantly, perhaps. A quick electrocution, a biomechanoid with
a rifle, a deadly force field.*

Nadia shuddered, but there was no other
choice than to see. It was this, or wait to be
hunted down like animals . . .

She closed her eyes for the briefest of seconds
and thought of Alexi. When she opened them,
the others were ready. Foster nodded to Steve,
who hit the latch swiftly and threw open the
door.

Nadia was in first, the others an instant behind
her. She leveled her weapon, her jaw clenched
in fear and fury, ready to blast at the mainframe—

—and blinked in utter shock. She shot a
glance at the others, saw the same stunned uncertainty mirrored there, then turned back to
where the computer should have been.

The room was empty. The main computer,
over four meters long and two thick, weighing
hundreds of kilos and towering well above a
man's head, was simply—gone. It had been
ripped from its mounts, had left behind only a
crater of ripped cable and torn decking. A single
tiny gatherer moved among the wires. Oblivious
to their presence, it seemed to be bundling the
useless cables in tiny, precise movements.

"It's gone," Nadia said softly.

Foster stared at the small robot, shaking her head. "Gone where?"

"The fucking thing *moved* itself," said Steve.

Nadia looked away from the bare wall, looked at the other three and saw that they were all thinking the same things, perhaps visualizing it as she was. A computer altered and transformed, dragging its massive bulk through the dead corridors, trailing its electrical roots behind. An animated monstrosity, seeking a dark corner in which to evolve . . .

Silently the four of them withdrew. They backed up the Cold Hall to the hatch, Nadia feeling a sudden overwhelming urgency to get away from the empty room, the empty deck. Something was wrong here, they had to get to a safe place and decide what to do next—

The hatch was closed and latched. Steve pulled up the handle, put his shoulder to the door—and it didn't move.

Nadia placed her hand against the inner seam and drew back quickly, the paint blistered and hot to the touch.

"Welded," said Steve.

Foster stared at him. "But we just came *through* there!"

They exchanged looks and Nadia turned, led them running back towards the computer room and past. Hiko just kept up with them as Nadia turned at a passage offshoot towards the science labs, to the next available exit.

Steve grabbed for the latch of the inset door, threw his weight against it almost frantically. Nadia's heart sank even as her pulse quickened, fingers clenched and sweaty against the weapon's stock. She could feel the heat still radiating from the seams of the hatch.

"It knows we're here," she said.

Steve turned away from the immovable door, his expression grim and horribly exhausted as he stated what they all knew now as irrefutable fact.

"We've been set up."

· 21 ·

Nadia led them through a dark and twisting maze of corridors that seemed to go on forever, making sudden turns and stops as they followed, helping Hiko as best they could. Steve hoped to God that she knew D well; he was completely lost, and each hatch they tried was either welded or blocked. If there was a way out, the Russian woman would have to take them to it—and he got the feeling that she was running out of ideas.

They stopped in front of another bulkhead hatch, Nadia pushing at the latch uselessly. Hiko was trying not to show it, but Steve could see the pain in his brown eyes, see him struggling not to apologize for slowing them up. Steve wished he could tell him that it was okay, but the circumstances didn't exactly warrant reassurance; *nothing* was okay.

Hiko looked away suddenly, tattooed nostrils flaring. "You smell something?"

Steve froze, recalling the biomechanoid at the engine room—and then they all heard it, just as the sickening odor of burnt and rotting flesh reached them. Multiple steps, heavy, grinding—coming closer.

The sounds resonated through the corridor behind them, making it nearly impossible to tell from which direction it came. They started backing away, weapons raised, Steve reflexively pushing the others behind him as they moved.

Please don't let it be Squeaky—

A glow, a yellow-green flashing glow, accompanied the thick stench and the crashing steps, coming from an offshoot to the right. Steve took a deep breath to control his rising terror—and then it stepped into view, and control was out of the question.

Like the one they'd seen before, the biomechanoid was at least seven feet tall and resembled nothing so much as a tremendous insect, a praying mantis—except its multiple legs were partly formed with raw, dripping muscle, its upper body made of skin and armor and flashing lights. Clutching mechanical arms were tipped with plierslike claws. Video lenses surrounded the misshapen "head," what looked like a mass of human brain tissue thickly wired with cables and metal plates. Heavy cables snaked off behind it.

It turned its lenses towards them, focused beams of blinding, sickly green light across them, and screeched—a shrill electronic squeal, inhuman, furious.

"Not good, mates, they're getting bigger,"

Hiko stammered, and then opened fire as the creature stomped heavily towards them.

"Power cables!" Steve shouted, and raised his shotgun, trying to get a clear shot.

"Aim for its cables!" Foster added, and then they were all firing as the seven-foot biomechanoid advanced amidst the thundering explosives.

Rounds ricocheted off the armor, the clever placement of the thick metal plates blocking the shots directed at the cables. Bullets flew wildly as the undamaged creature continued towards them.

One of the shots slammed into an overhead pipe, and suddenly the freakish monster was enveloped in a hissing cloud of steam. Steve jammed more rounds into his shotgun and blasted again and again as the other three unloaded their clips into the thing. The corridor was flooding with steam and water from burst pipes and the creature came on, barely slowed by the barrage of fire.

Foster's empty magazine clattered to the deck next to Hiko's.

"Is there a plan B?" Foster shouted.

They had backed up past a side corridor and Steve pointed, still firing the shotgun. Foster grabbed Hiko and then they were all running for it, down the dark offshoot and away from the relentlessly approaching biomechanism.

There weren't any hatches in the offshoot, and Steve realized his mistake even as he saw the blank bulkhead in front of them. It was a dead end.

Who the fuck would put an empty hall goin' nowhere on a ship?

The creature had reached the entrance to the

corridor just as Nadia frantically gestured towards one corner. Steve followed the motion, then saw what he'd missed in his panic. A ladder, the rungs leading up into a vertical maintenance tunnel.

"Where does it go?" Foster gasped.

"I don't know," said Nadia.

The creature started down the corridor towards them.

"I don't care!" Steve shouted. "Climb!"

Nadia went first, Hiko behind her, then Foster. Steve clambered up after them, praying that the creature wouldn't make the ladder before they got far enough out of its reach. The scuttle was too narrow for it to follow—

There was a hideous shriek directly beneath him and the wall shook. Steve heard rending metal, risked a look down, and saw steel claws destroy the bolted rungs below, slice through them with incredible ease.

He heard Foster cry out as the ladder trembled, as she slipped suddenly. He reached up and caught her leg. She steadied herself and continued to climb.

The creature screeched again in a seeming frenzy of rage—but they had cleared its deadly grasp and found a way out of the trap that had been set for them.

Steve wished that this meant they were safe, but knew better. He swallowed, hard, and followed the others into territories unknown.

■ ■ ■

Richie sat cross-legged on the floor of the missile room, counting out lengths of cable and reveling in his heightened awareness. He'd smoked some more shit to fully appreciate his newfound sense of purpose and he now realized that nothing could touch him. It wasn't that he was invulnerable, it was just that he was so—*in tune* that he was ready for anything.

"... human brain can hold more than a hundred computers," he mumbled, "ain't gettin' mine. Getting out, I gotta *plan* ..."

The beginning of the end. He was going to have to run an errand or two to insure the success of his operation, but that was okay; he was looking forward to it.

Me and you, baby; won't be any fun if I don't get to see a little action!

The slightly altered fuse lay next to him, wired for sound—not to mention the multipoint hook he'd rigged that would allow him to detonate every warhead in the room with the single trigger. The uncased warheads themselves were a safe distance away, their fuses detached; he didn't want any little accidents before the time was right ...

He measured out the last of the cable and set it against a spool of nylon rope he'd found in a footlocker beneath the missile rack. All told, he had 250 feet, give or take—but that was including the light nylon, which he didn't really want to use, and it wasn't going to be near enough for what he had in mind.

"It thinks it's smarter than me? Sure. Gonna get a surprise ..."

He stood and stretched leisurely, grinning, and wondered if the others were still alive. Maybe he'd see them on his expedition—

—*or maybe I'll see* parts *of them, anyway.*

His grin faded. That wasn't so funny. Squeaky had been a good guy, he hadn't deserved what had happened to him—and just because Richie had a plan and the rest of them didn't, that didn't mean he wanted to see them end up like Squeak.

But I'll be takin' care of that too, won't I?

Richie smiled again, a tight, urgent smile as he thought of how it was gonna be.

"Beautiful," he whispered, and went to get ready for his trip into the jungle, still smiling.

■ ■ ■

Everton made his way down through the *Volkov,* trying to prepare himself for the meeting. He hadn't been attacked or stopped, although he'd heard things skittering through the shadows on his way to the stairwell—and twice he'd smelled the putrescent odor of rotting flesh drifting towards him through the corridors.

He caught a whiff of it now as he stepped through the bulkhead hatch and onto E deck. The alien creature had been considerate enough to light his path, making it clear which corridors to take; it was still dim and flickering, but it was obvious he was headed in the right direction . . .

Go back, don't do this . . .

Everton shook off the quietly nagging voice that had followed him all the way from C deck, scowling. Nerves. He was uneasy, true, but he wasn't about to let simple apprehension stop him from cutting a deal; this meeting was the answer to everything. If things went well, they'd make it to port, he'd inform the proper authorities, and they would clear the *Volkov* of its alien guest;

the ship would probably sustain further damage, but his salvage would still be solid—and as the sole survivor of an alien encounter at sea, he could write his own ticket while he waited for the lien to clear the courts.

And all that aside, there's the little matter of my survival to consider. I don't have a choice here; anyone can see that.

He turned to the right at the end of the corridor and stopped cold. Halfway down the hall was the source of the foul air—and a thing that hurt his mind to see, a monstrosity from a madman's nightmare. He hadn't gotten a clear look at the one that had killed Woods; things had been happening too fast . . .

Tall, easily seven or eight feet. Four mechanical legs squatted beneath an armored torso; four arms, two human and two that were not, set at right angles to one another at midchest, interspersed with glowing lights. Crowning the horror were three human brains, fitted with optical lenses and crisscrossed with shining wire.

The lenses that he could see hummed and ticked, focusing on him, but the creature held perfectly still. He realized that it was a sentry, a guard for the workshop where he was expected. He swallowed his rising gorge and forced himself to walk towards it. He had already made his decision.

As he approached the freakish hybrid, it reached back with one metal arm and pulled open the door behind it. The arm moved, but the rest of the terrible body remained still, watching him.

Everton stepped to the entry, keeping as far away as possible from the guard and holding his breath against the fetid stench. He nodded towards it, trying to seem authoritative and composed, a man on business—but he couldn't look at it, and just standing so close to such a thing, he felt his determination slipping.

Don't go in!

It was too late; even if he *wanted* to leave, the creature would surely stop him. The *Volkov* rumbled around him, shaken by another distant wave. Everton squared his shoulders and walked in.

The workroom was dimly lit, the air heavy with rot and machine oil and other scents he couldn't name. Most of the light came from three computer screens against the back wall, illuminating a series of long, low tables and the—things that worked at them. Things like Squeaky had been, like the Russian on the bridge—and variations of the two that had Everton struggling not to run screaming, regardless of the consequences.

There were occasional bursts of brilliant light from the welding torches that some of them held, casting strobing flashes across the bodies and circuitry they worked over. He saw an expressionless male biomechanoid with four hands at one table, threading torn slabs of muscle tissue with wire filaments. At another was the upper chest and head of a male corpse on its side, a biomechanoid with lenses instead of eyes drilling at its exposed spine.

Everton swallowed heavily and started for the computers, moving carefully between the rows of workbenches where body parts and huge tangles of wire and unfamiliar components were stacked and piled. He passed a biomechanoid that was wiring the belly of its own twin; soft, wet, meaty sounds hung in the air as the creature dug through the cold flesh.

Just stay calm, say your piece, don't upset it.

He reached the humming consoles, all thoughts of trying to drive a hard bargain completely lost. Getting out of this alive was all he wanted, and he'd do whatever the alien being asked of him to manage it. He had to make it see that he could be useful, could—help it to trap the others, take it to any port, *anything.*

"They're trying to destroy you," he said, not caring that his voice shook, that he was no longer the man who had walked into this nightmare with his head held high. "But you know that, don't you . . . ?"

There was a noise behind him and Everton whipped his head around, saw another biomechanoid stir to life. This one had a human head— except for the camera lens that was grafted into the left side of its face, which turned towards him with a mechanical whir. A light set next to the lens went on, the yellowish beam striking Everton.

He turned back to the computers, searching desperately for something more to say, something to stop the fear inside that was threatening to swallow him up.

I'm a captain, I—I can do whatever you want; don't you see, I HAVE NO CHOICE.

A half-dissected human torso on the table nearest him slowly sat up, swiveling towards him, oozing fluids dripping from the open cavity of its chest. It had been decapitated, the stump of the neck jagged with flaps of skin and tissue, the gleaming white of crushed vertebrae protruding from the mass of gore.

Everton's sickened, terrified gaze fell to the table, saw that the head of the corpse sat next to the body—and that it was Woods. The helmsman's eyes were open and glazed with death, but even as Everton stared, the dead gaze of his crewman seemed to fix on his own. A pathetic, pleading look that secured Everton's horrified silence with the truth of the matter.

He had made a mistake.

The heavy door to the workshop closed gently and Everton started to scream.

· 22 ·

Hiko managed the cold steel rungs in front of him for what seemed like forever, limbs trembling with fear and exhaustion. He felt the beat of his heart throbbing in the torn flesh of his leg, each flex of the muscle a fresh burst of pain.

He tried to think of a prayer as they ascended the scuttle, but all he could think of was the song about the three baskets of life that his *kuia* used to sing to him and his sister after his parents had died, the soothing lilt of her voice sending them off to sleep. He gave up praying and thought of his grandmother instead, and his parents. He'd be joining them soon.

The terrible screams of the monster had fallen away, but had been replaced by a roaring that grew in strength as they climbed higher. Hiko dreaded the sound, feared it more than the creature they'd faced below—but he'd known all along, deep down, that this was how it would be.

"Wait," Nadia called, and they stopped while she fumbled at a latch in the darkness.

The Russian grunted with exertion and threw the hatch open. The roar of the *Tawhirimatea* enveloped them, cold rain and wild, screaming wind tearing through the scuttle. They had reached the top deck of the *Volkov*.

Hiko felt the weight of the war club against his hip and tried to accept how it was—but he couldn't. He was going to die at the claws of a furious sea, eager to claim him after waiting for so long, and he was terrified.

Nadia pulled herself up and reached down to help him. Hiko wondered why the vicious storm hadn't ripped her away and saw that the maintenance tunnel was covered, at least partly. It was the satellite dish, the one that had fallen to the deck; the giant antenna acted as a shield against the worst of the violent winds.

He limped onto the thundering deck, helped Nadia hold the hatch open as Foster and Steve crawled out. The railing around the exit had been mostly crushed by the massive dish, but there was enough for them to steady themselves against the lashing typhoon—at least for the moment.

Hiko looked out at the giant swells of the ocean and saw only death. Tons of *Tangaroa* surged up, tossing and rocking the ship, crashing against the bow, and calling his name. It was worse than his worst nightmare, the battering waves thrashing over the open deck beneath a black and boiling sky.

Nadia pointed up, yelling to be heard over the raging storm.

"The antenna control room! We'll be safe there!"

Hiko looked up, saw the glassed box that she meant, and shook his head, gripping the railing as another hundred tons of foaming death slammed into the hull of the ship. They'd never make it, *he'd* never make it. He curled his arm around the pipe, touched his *wahaika*, and closed his eyes.

"What's his problem?" Foster called.

"He's afraid of water!" Steve answered.

"Hiko—?"

He opened his eyes, saw Foster and the others staring at him, saw sympathy and disbelief.

"I—I can't swim!"

"Hiko, your greatest fear, remember! You gotta face it! *You won't die!*"

Hiko looked at Steve, took a deep breath, and nodded once. He didn't know if he would survive, but he wasn't going to shame himself by cowering and whining like a child, forcing these people to drag him away from the railing.

They started across the sea-washed deck, edging towards the mounted ladder that would take them to the antenna room against the gusting winds. Hiko refused to look at the churning, angry water that surrounded them, knew that it would be the last thing he saw if he allowed himself to look. Rain bit into his skin, bruising his tired flesh as he stared down at his feet, the *wahaika* clutched in one trembling hand.

Steve screamed back at him, urging him on. "Twenty more feet to that ladder! Climb up to the door! Real simple!"

Hiko glanced up, unable to believe that they were that close—and saw that it was true.

The *wahaika* was going to save him. Hiko started to grin, the stone suddenly warm beneath his fingers, its power coursing through him. It was true, his grandfather was right, he wasn't going to die—

The ship keeled suddenly into a trough and Steve fell to the deck, water sloshing across him and piling him into Foster. She lost her balance, flailed wildly before falling next to him.

Hiko didn't stop to think about it. He limped forward and knelt, helped Steve to his feet and let Foster balance against his crouched form. When the two of them were stable, he stood up and they continued on.

Nadia reached the ladder first and started to climb. The others made it to the dripping rungs and Foster went up next, Steve meeting Hiko's surprised gaze with a tight grin before he followed.

The touch of the wet metal filled Hiko with an almost violent relief. He tucked the *wahaika* into his belt with numb fingers and started up after them, delirious with joy and a newfound hope; if the *Tangaroa* could not hurt him, anything was possible. Maybe there was a way to thwart the evil that had taken over the Russian *wakataua,* for all of them to make it to safe waters alive and—

—and from the deck below, a door exploded open, torn off its hinges by the seven foot monster that stepped out onto the heaving deck and started for them.

■ ■ ■

Foster heard the crash of metal, saw the thick metal hatch break through the railing and disappear beneath the thrashing waves. Her stomach knotted as she opened her mouth to scream a warning—

—and a giant metal fist crashed into the steel plating only inches from her face, puncturing the solid metal as if it were paper.

Foster screamed, half turning—and caught sight of the monstrous creature through the whipping curtain of rain, the multiple legs and arms moving smoothly beneath the pulsing lights of its human brain.

The towering biomechanoid lunged forward as she scrabbled at the rungs. It tore at the ladder, bolts snapping as it jerked, hard—

Foster screamed again as the rung slipped from her hands, wind and rain howling with her as she fell—

—and warm, muscular arms caught her awkwardly, gripping her tight against the clutches of gravity and the brutal gusts of wind.

Hiko!

Foster managed to find her balance as the Maori boosted her into Steve's reaching grasp. She caught just a glimpse of Hiko's face, his eyes flashing with anger and disgust, before Steve wrapped an arm around her and lifted her up.

Hiko screamed something in his native tongue, the words foreign but the meaning crystal clear as he jerked his club from his belt. His powerful war cry thundered over the crash of waves as he leapt away from the ladder and onto the creature's mutant body. With a scream of fury, Hiko buried his weapon in the biomechanoid's gelid brain.

Sparks flew as the creature spasmed, its limbs flailing wildly. Hiko yanked his war club out of the pulpy mass and struck again and again, slashing at the power cables of the thing's spine in a frenzy of rage.

Clinging to the wet rungs, the three of them started shouting for Hiko to get away as a sudden burst of lightning illuminated the terrible scene below. Hiko didn't let up, pounding at whatever he could reach. Blood and circuitry flashed amidst the relentless waves of rain, and the massive biomechanoid turned, its legs sliding on the slick deck as it struggled brokenly to get back to the open hatch.

My God, he's killing *it!*

A massive clap of thunder shook the *Volkov* and both Hiko and the staggering giant fell to the deck, Hiko still slashing and pounding. Flesh and bone were smashed, wires spitting out sparks, metal twisting beneath the tribal club—

—and a huge swell crashed over the deck, tons of water driving Hiko and the faltering creature against the shattered railing. The biomechanoid skidded wildly out into the turbulent sea and disappeared.

"Hiko!" Foster screamed, watching helplessly as the stunned deck hand struggled to hang on to the side of the ship, his dripping club still gripped in one hand.

Foster saw the second massive wave only a split second before it hit.

NO!

When the foaming water poured off of the *Volkov*'s quaking deck, Hiko was gone.

After what seemed like an eternity, Steve

looked up at her, and she at Nadia. There was nothing they could do except climb.

Nadia crawled off the ladder and braced her legs against the top rung, helping Foster up with one cold, strong hand. They both gripped at Steve's shirt, pulling him up, and the three of them opened the door to the control room and staggered inside.

Steve slammed the door, and Foster felt almost deafened by the sudden quiet. They were in a large, shadowy room, consoles and charts lining every wall except where hatches were inset, leading to another area. Storage, probably . . .

Foster walked to a window, stared down at the stormy waters below.

"We lost him," Steve said.

Foster watched the churning sea and felt a lump rise in her throat. "Maybe he made it to another part of the ship—"

Steve sounded almost angry. "Not a chance. So much for facing your greatest fear."

"Hiko saved our lives," she said softly, then turned to look at the others. Nadia had already disabled the surveillance camera and moved to the fore window, arms crossed tightly, her expression troubled. Steve had unshouldered his bag and was digging through it with shaking hands, obviously upset. Her and Hiko's empty semiautomatics and a few handfuls of loose rounds fell across the table. He pulled out his flashlight, checked it, then his walkie-talkie.

"Walkie still works," he said, then dropped it back into the bag and stared down blankly at the table.

Foster looked around the room aimlessly and

saw the rack of emergency equipment by the entry—a fire ax and extinguisher, next to a half dozen life jackets hanging from a bar. Hanging there uselessly, when Hiko was dead, unable to swim at all. Without one, he'd had no chance . . .

Nadia turned away from the window, frowning. "It *is* steering the ship."

Foster nodded. It had to be, or the *Volkov* wouldn't have made it this far. She reached for her compass, then saw that there was one bolted to a chart table near Nadia. She walked over, checked their heading, and then studied the chart. It was of the South Pacific.

"It's not just steering, it's *navigating*," she said, and traced her finger across the paper, stopping at a tiny speck. She couldn't read Russian, but she knew what she was looking at. "Lord Howe Island."

Steve frowned. "It's just a small island, there's nothing there—"

Nadia stared up at them, eyes wide. "There's a British Intelligence station there. They have digital linkups to every military and commercial satellite in the Southern Hemisphere . . ."

Foster's heart was sinking. "If it gets into a communications satellite or the transoceanic Pacific—it could go *anywhere*."

There was a tense silence as they stared at one another in the swaying room. It was broken by a burst of static from one of the consoles.

They all whirled around, startled, as a man's voice crackled into the control room over the ship-to-ship.

"This is the NOAA Research Vessel *Norfolk* transmitting in the clear to unknown vessel. Received Mayday from your position at oh eight-twenty hours, we have you on radar."

Jesus, Richie's Mayday got through!

"Is this Research Vessel *Vladislav Volkov*? Is your vessel in distress? If you are receiving but cannot transmit, please respond by rocket or flare, over . . ."

Steve turned to them excitedly. "We need a flare gun—"

"No," said Nadia quietly. She walked to the radio and turned it off. Steve stared at her, astonished. Nadia went on, her voice weary and sad.

"If anything, we need to warn them away."

Foster nodded slowly. "She's right. This thing is isolated here on this ship; it views the human race as its own personal organ donor. We can't let another ship near us."

Steve closed his eyes and sank to the floor. He looked up at them, and Foster saw how exhausted he was, how very, very tired.

"We have to sink this ship," he said.

No one spoke for a long moment. Foster opened her mouth, not sure what she was going to say until it came out.

"How?"

Nadia reached into her satchel and pulled out a thermite grenade, looking between the two of them with a troubled gaze. Troubled but resolute.

"Flood the hold with fuel and detonate it."

Steve nodded. "Works for me."

"One more question," said Foster. "How do we survive?"

Nadia put the grenade back in her waist bag, staring down at her hands. Steve met her gaze evenly, forcing a half smile onto his weary face.

He shrugged, and she found herself smiling back at him.

They wouldn't make it. She'd known before she had even asked, but couldn't stop herself from hoping that maybe one of them had some miracle in mind—

The air stirred and Foster turned, saw that the hatch into the storage room had come open. There was a man standing there, silhouetted by a light behind him, but Foster recognized the shape, the scruffy, weathered outline of his face— and she was almost glad to see him, to see that he was still alive.

"Captain Everton!" she said, amazed that he had gotten here on his own, that he had escaped the creature—

—and then he stepped forward, and she realized that he hadn't escaped at all.

· 23 ·

The thing that had been Captain Everton stepped out of the shadows of the storage room, trailing a power cable behind it. They stared at him, shocked into silence by the grotesque thing that he had become.

Nadia felt her heart twist and shrivel in her chest; the intelligence had done to him what it had done to poor Alexi. Half of Everton's skull was peeled back, a viscous blue gel surrounding his exposed brain; twisted ropes of wire lay across the glistening tissue. His upper body seemed otherwise untouched, but his legs had been dramatically altered—thick plates of metal covered the fronts and sides, riveted through muscle and into bone. She could see cords woven through and around the plates, hear the click and whir of circuitry as he moved into the room.

Foster backed away, her eyes wide and terrified. Everton turned his head towards her, the movement strange and unnatural, a machine tracking motion.

"Foster, don't you know me? It's me, Bob, your captain."

The intelligence had gotten better at simulating humanity; he, *it* sounded almost the same as the captain had before. Nadia looked around desperately for a weapon, but she'd discarded the empty rifle below, there'd been no more ammo. Steve was fumbling through his pack for a clip and rounds as Everton stepped forward, his expression a caricature of hurt curiosity.

"Is something wrong?"

Foster snatched up a chair and swung it around, connected with his face so solidly that the supports snapped. Everton barely flinched as the pieces clattered to the floor, as blood began to pulse from a tear beneath his right eye socket.

The captain's arm came up and he backhanded her, dropped her sprawling to the deck. His lips curled back with rage, revealing crimson teeth.

"I'm your captain! You will treat me with respect!"

Steve had dropped the bullets. He ran to the door and grabbed the fire ax, then wheeled around and rushed at the captain. Foster scrambled to her feet and lunged for the pistol.

The hollow *thunk* of the ax blade penetrating Everton's sternum was sickening, the metal wedged tightly. The biomechanoid looked down at the half-submerged blade with blank eyes, assimilating the information.

Steve backed away to where Foster stood. She

jammed a partly loaded magazine into the .32 and pointed it at Everton.

"We know where you're going," she said.

Everton looked up and spoke tonelessly now, the voice of the intelligence with no pretense of emotion. "I know you do."

The creature reached up and gripped the handle of the ax. With a single easy pull, the blade slipped out and Everton hefted it into both hands.

"There's a whole world waiting out there," it said.

Foster fired and bone and tissue flew from between the captain's eyes. Wire flopped out across the waxy forehead, hissing and twisting as trickles of the blue fluid ran down the thin metal.

"That hurts," it muttered, then stepped towards Foster again.

She lowered her aim and emptied the clip, five more explosive shots that splashed into Everton's chest in a steady rhythm. The biomechanoid walked steadily into the small-caliber rounds, gripping the ax loosely.

Its back was to Nadia. She saw the tangled river of wires that connected to the spine from the power cable and knew what to do.

She snatched a thermite grenade from her bag and stepped forward, pulling the pin in the same fluid motion.

She stuffed the explosive into the thickening of the wires and screamed at the same time.

"Steve, Foster, GET BACK!"

Before she could dive for cover, Steve tackled the biomechanoid, low. He drove the captain backwards and through the open hatch to the

storage room, then pushed himself off of the un-
balanced Everton.

The creature fell down in the second room as
Steve leapt past a console and ducked next to
Foster. Nadia took one running step and dove
into a crouch behind the chart table.

The explosion shook the control room, as-
sorted shrapnel whizzing overhead, and the creature started to scream, a screeching, human
counterpart to the electronic squeal of the intelligence. Foul, chemical-scented smoke poured
into the room, aluminum and iron oxide tainted
with burning flesh.

Nadia stood, saw Foster and Steve rise and
watch.

Everton was flailing wildly, had flipped onto
its side as the white-hot cinders erupted from the
back; the thermite plasma had melted through
its spine, but it still shrieked, thrashed, threw
sparks from the liquefying circuitry.

The molten heat was burning through the deck
as Everton divided, the abdomen gone. Still, the
legs kicked, the furious mask howled its eerie cry
as the widening hole opened up beneath the
creature.

Bones snapped as the Everton-thing convulsed
and spasmed, metals burning, white smoke
clouding up and filling the smaller room. With a
final cracking *crash* the deck gave way—and the
captain disappeared, plunged through the smoking hole and into the raging darkness below.

The thundering of the storm was a blessed silence. Steve and Foster edged cautiously towards
the hole, Nadia stepping out to join them.

"How's *that* for respect, Captain?" Steve whispered.

Everton was gone—but how much had the intelligence heard and seen? Nadia turned to them and spoke quickly.

"Listen—through your captain it knows what we are planning."

Steve stared down at the black, storming winds below. "I never did like that guy . . ."

Foster moved back into the control room and scooped up three life jackets, tossing one to each of them as Steve slung his bag and Nadia tied on her pack.

Nadia touched her dog tags lightly and hoped that they would make it in time—and that Alexi would be waiting for her when it was all over.

■ ■ ■

They worked their way down the aft emergency scuttle that Nadia had led them to, a thin, dark passage that would take them straight to the fuel oil bay.

Flood the hold, set the timer, and get as far away as we can . . .

Steve wished they had more time to work out the details of their plan, but the creature wasn't going to wait for them to catch up. He didn't want to think about what it was up to as they hurried down the scuttle—but he didn't imagine it was going to stand by idly and watch them destroy the ship.

He called up to Nadia, past Foster. "How do we know we're not gonna get welded in down there?"

"This way there are no corridors, no doors—nothing to weld," she answered. Her voice was strained with exhaustion, but she sounded certain.

Steve hoped she was right; although they stood little chance against the storm, he preferred drowning to going up in a fireball. They'd blow the *Volkov* either way, there wasn't really a choice there—but if he was going to die, he'd rather not have it be in a biomechanical death trap, running from some stinking monster.

His foot hit air and Steve dropped the four feet from the last rung to the corridor. He reached up and slipped his hands around Foster's slender waist, helping her down—and was surprised by the rush of emotions he felt, just touching her. Regret, sadness, admiration . . . lust.

Steve shook his head. If there could possibly be a more inappropriate time or place, he couldn't think of it. Normal reaction, he supposed—there hadn't been a chance for him to catch his breath since they'd boarded the ship, for him to work out his feelings over Squeaky and the others who had died, even Everton. It was all just catching up to him and he hadn't slept more than an hour in the last twenty-four—

—*and she's an incredible woman, and ain't life a bitch.*

They quickly helped Nadia down and Steve turned his flashlight on and aimed it through the rungs—

—and they all gasped, Steve so startled that he nearly dropped the light. A man, only a few feet away—

—*Richie?*

"Richie, you scared the shit out of us!" Foster said.

The deckhand's face was covered with black grease, what Steve realized was a homemade camouflage. Night vision goggles were propped up on his forehead and he carried two giant coils of cable, one over each shoulder—as well as an AK-47 which he raised towards them, the whites of his eyes rolling wildly.

The three of them backed up a step; Richie looked completely insane.

"Richie, it's us," Foster said slowly.

"How do I know that?" Richie snapped, his demented gaze flickering between Foster and Steve.

They didn't have time for this; Steve cut to the chase.

"We're blowin the ship. Come with us."

Richie lowered the rifle, apparently satisfied that they were human. He grinned suddenly, a flash of white against his blackened skin.

"Don't worry about me," he said, and started backing down the corridor.

"Richie, don't be a fool!" Foster shouted, but he wasn't listening. He pulled down his goggles and turned, disappearing into the darkness.

Steve looked at the two women and shook his head. At least they had been able to tell him what they were going to do—what they were going to *try* to do. If he didn't want to help, they couldn't make him; Steve just hoped that he was planning on an evacuation of his own . . .

Nadia started towards a hatch and they followed, Steve still wondering what Richie was planning—and what the creature would throw at them when it realized that it was almost over.

■ ■ ■

The ladder that stretched above him was clear as day, the rungs glowing soft green through the night vision goggles. Richie worked his way up as quickly as possible, lugging the heavy cables that he'd found back on E.

He'd been surprised to see Steve and the two women, he wouldn't have guessed that they'd survive this long—but he was even more surprised that he'd been sorry not to see Hiko with them. He didn't give much of a shit about Everton, but Hiko hadn't been some money-grubbing fuckhead. A little freaky-looking maybe, but a decent guy . . .

He shook the thoughts as he reached the entry to C deck. He'd left the hatch open and he leaned out into the corridor and gave it a thorough look before throwing out the cable; all clear.

He started back towards the weapons locker, moving carefully but not as slow as he'd gone before. If the other three were going to blow the ship and they were down on E, they probably meant to ignite the fuel oil, probably on some kind of timer. He hoped they got out before his own little surprise; he had enough cable now, the warheads were stacked—he was gonna depart this hellhole with a great, big bang, and he was going to do it as soon as he got back and hooked up the grenades—

Richie turned a corner in the hallway and froze. There was a body on the floor not twenty feet in front of him, and there was a power cable coming out of its back.

He could smell it now, the same rotten odor that came from all the biomechanisms—or at least the ones made out of Russians. He trained the AK-47 on the still figure, but it didn't move.

A trap, some kinda lure?

He didn't think so. The alien hadn't been particularly subtle so far, it didn't *need* to be . . .

He kept his rifle on the downed biomechanoid just to be on the safe side and started to edge around it, prepared to blast if it so much as coughed—and stopped suddenly, listening.

He was in the corridor near the workshop, where he and Woods had first seen the tiny 'droids. When he'd passed it on his way down to E, it had been humming and clicking, the little bastards still plugging away. Now there wasn't a sound from that direction. In fact, there was no sound *anywhere*—the *Volkov* had been quiet before, but there had been the constant, faint vibrations of machinery at work, of computers and lights and video systems in operation.

Richie turned, sought out the closest video surveillance camera; it was dead, all right, no little red light, no tracking. He realized that he could still feel the shift of air, the ventilation was working, which meant the engines were still on—but everything that the alien had taken over was dead, as dead as the Russian corpse-machine in front of him.

Why would it do that? Why would the alien suddenly turn everything off, like it was—

Like it was drawing up all its power for something else.

Richie took off running, really scared for the first time since he'd left the missile room. It was time to get out. Now.

● ● ●

All across the ship, the machines were dying. In the thick shadows of the corridors, behind

welded metal doors, crawling between decks—
lights dimmed and limbs froze into position as
their enegy source drained away, their strange
bodies slumping and falling where they stood.
An eerie, pensive silence swept over the lifeless
halls and dark chambers of the *Volkov* as power
surged away from the creatures, robbing them of
purpose—and funneled towards the machine
room on E deck, rushing soundlessly to the giant
computer that controlled the ship.

The mainframe welcomed the massive incom-
ing flux of alien life, wires heating and lights
flashing, information whipping through stimu-
lated circuits. The computer fed obediently, taking the energy in and manipulating it, refocusing
it for its final destination.

Arcs of electricity snapped through the air as
the intelligence moved from the mainframe
through a massive, bloated cable strung across
the room. The cable jumped as the creature
pulsed through, its power swarming towards the
form that was its own creation. Sparks showered
and flew against the rising hum of new life.

Steel and bone arched and flexed. Flesh and
metal sang as the intelligence flowed into the
powerful armature that it had designed and built
as its ultimate home.

The mainframe went dark, the last of its lights
fading out, its task complete.

The intelligence was embodied in something
new.

It lived.

· 24 ·

Nadia had hooked up the timer after they'd opened the valves, all three of them nervously waiting while the ballast tanks emptied, each spout blasting fuel oil at over a hundred gallons a second. They could hear the splashing below, through an open ladder well in the far corner of the bay. After a few minutes, Nadia nodded at them and Steve picked up the grenade.

Foster watched him set the detonator and attach it and the thermite grenade to a row of pipes that ran below the valve wheels, just out of sight. When it detonated, the deadly plasma would burn through the deck at something like three thousand degrees centigrade, plunging through to the flooded hold below . . .

"I gave us fifteen minutes," he said.

"Checkmate," said Nadia softly.

Foster took a deep breath, nodding. There was no going back now. She snapped into her life jacket quickly and moved to check Steve's, then Nadia's while Steve tugged against hers. It was time to face the storm—and while she wasn't looking forward to it, nothing could be worse than what they'd discovered on the *Volkov*.

They were walking towards the hatch when Foster heard it. She stopped, turned, and saw that both Steve and Nadia were listening as well, eyes wide.

A heavy booming. Metal pounding against metal, and it was coming from outside the bay, close—and getting closer at an incredible speed.

They backed away, all three of them looking for another way out—but there was only the hatch and the cargo door, and the ladders that led down into the hold. Nowhere to go, to get away—

The booming stopped in front of the cargo door.

Before they could take another step, there was a massive strike against the huge steel door, a blow that crashed through the metal and ripped half of it down in a single motion.

Even partly revealed, it took her breath away. A mammoth armature, twelve feet tall, an abhorrent mixture of flesh, bone, and steel. Dancing arcs of blue electricity pulsed across its form, snapped and crackled.

Another thundering blow and the cargo door was torn completely away. Foster saw four arms, four legs—all of them hydraulic at the joints but made up of stretched muscle tissue and flesh, riveted metal and wire. A huge, blocky head of murkily glowing lenses and what looked like insect mandibles, although there was no mouth.

Goliath, thought Foster, and then it slammed its way into the bay.

"It has evolved," Nadia whispered.

Steve unslung his pack and the creature stepped forward and lashed out with one giant arm. The blow knocked Steve across the room and into one wall, where he crumpled—and didn't move.

Foster started to scream, heard Nadia join her, and the two of them ran for cover as Goliath turned to seek them out.

■ ■ ■

Richie stood on the launch platform in the missile room and surveyed his handiwork, eager to be on his way. Over five hundred feet of cable lay coiled up between the escape seat and the explosives; he'd rigged up the perfect solution to the problem of alien invasion, if he did say so himself.

There were twenty uncased warheads grouped on the deck, with a half dozen thermite grenades duct-taped on top. The fuse hookup was attached to one end of the cable. All that was left was to strap himself into the chair and ignite the rocket motor, which would also open the launch doors. When he hit the button, he'd become a space cowboy—and the cable would pull tight, trigger the fuse-VT, and blow the fuck out of ol' Visitor in an explosion that would put the typhoon to shame.

The walkie-talkie suddenly spat to life over by his bag of stuff—and screams filled the missile room, frantic, terrified, wordless cries. Female.

"Who's a fool now, Foster?" Richie said, but it didn't feel as satisfying as he thought it would. He wondered who was pushing the transmit button; it sure as hell couldn't be Foster or that Russian, they were both howling their damn heads off . . .

. . . and maybe he was a fool, after all. Because he wasn't picking up his shit and strapping into the chair, the way he should've been. Instead, he stood there listening to two women he didn't even care about shrieking in mortal terror—and he was starting to feel a little . . . strange about it. He hadn't needed them, that was for certain. But maybe *they* had needed *him;* maybe if he had stayed with them, they wouldn't be screaming right now.

Richie snarled at himself and started gathering up his stuff; there was nothing he could do for them except what he already had planned. The sooner he got outta here, the sooner they'd shut up—and the sooner he could stop feeling the strange, unpleasant feelings that were hammering at his guts, telling him maybe he wasn't such a good guy.

■ ■ ■

Oh, Steve, NO—!

He was unconscious or dead, his unmoving body huddled over his pack, his life jacket shredded—but there was no time to check, no way to get to him; Goliath had fixed on them.

Foster and Nadia ran, took cover behind a steel support beam that bisected the fuel bay. Goliath took a single step forward, raised one massive arm—

—and backhanded the steel beam with such force that the six inches of metal snapped in a rending thunder. Both women were knocked back, slid across the deck—

—and into an open ladder well. Foster reached out in desperation, fingers scrabbling wildly as she plummeted. She caught on to a rung and her arm jerked painfully in its socket. She managed to hold on, barely, legs kicking in open air.

Nadia didn't grab on in time. She hit Foster on her way down, deflected off of her and landed somewhere below with a solid *thump*. Her scream cut off short, a final frantic resonation pulsing through the darkness.

Foster reached up, caught the rung with both hands, and looked down. Nothing but blackness and the heavy, greasy smell of fuel oil. Above, she heard the monstrous creature ripping the bay apart, the crash of metal and the hiss of steam, pipes torn and burst by the furious rampage of the machine . . .

She tried to pull herself up, but it was no good. She was exhausted, her overused muscles aching and quivering, her hands slick with sweat. She was slipping, and she just had time to relax, go limp before the rung escaped her grasp.

She fell. Thick air whipped past her face and she squeezed her eyes closed, prayed that she was above the viscous liquid—

—and she hit the lake of fuel oil with a tremendous splash, plunged under and bobbed to the surface, choking. The cool, sticky fluid coated her hair, her face, dribbled across a thousand tiny cuts, burning and stinging. She rubbed at her eyes, disoriented, saw that there was light coming from somewhere as something brushed past her in the syrupy ooze.

Foster pushed away, panicked—and into another bobbing object, and another. She could hear the lap of oil against them, against many more of the unknown objects, surrounding her. She stopped flailing, let the life jacket hold her steady as her eyes adjusted to the murky gloom.

The light was from somewhere overhead, a single shaded fluorescent that illuminated a catwalk high above and filtered down to the shadowy lake, showing her—

Foster screamed, unable to help it, her body thrashing of its own accord to get out, get away from the nightmare that she could barely see. Dozens of bodies floated on the sticky surface; the corpses of the Russian crew bobbed all around her, pale, dead skin gleaming through the shining oil. Everywhere she turned she saw matted hair, groping, lifeless fingers, blind eyes covered with dark and gleaming fluid.

Suddenly she heard it, heard the splashing of something huge somewhere in the dark, moving towards her. The panic intensified, all rational thought lost as Foster rolled over, kicking, trying to swim through the corpse-infested fuel oil.

She heard and felt the thick, clammy waves of oil push against her, the bodies of the Russian crew tossed aside as Goliath came for her. A screaming filled her ears, her own voice echoing back at her through the vast hold and urging her to new heights of terror as she paddled wildly. Pallid bodies pressed against her, bloodless lips yawning, contorted death masks and cold, outstretched hands brushing her skin—

—and a huge, frigid talon closed around her

ankle and ripped her backwards, dragging her through the oil. Her face was submerged. She struggled, managed one choking mouthful of air before her head was plunged forward again and she couldn't breathe, couldn't raise her head, which had grown heavy, heart pounding and lungs dying . . .

The blackness overtook her and Foster knew no more.

• 25 •

Nadia was standing in a room she couldn't quite see; she had an impression of softness and white in the flickering shadows, but the dimensions of the space distorted past her immediate surroundings, faded off into a vague distance.

She didn't know where she was or what had brought her here. Her thoughts were jumbled, confused. Something had happened, but she couldn't fix on what it was—and yet she wasn't afraid, not in this soft, peaceful place where no one was screaming—

—*screaming? Why would anyone be screaming?*

She had a memory of being very tired and shook off the troubling thought, relieved. The vagueness of the room suddenly made sense; she was asleep.

"Nadia."

A familiar voice, deep and compelling. She turned and felt her eyes well with tears, suddenly overwhelmed with happiness. Alexi Sagalevitch stood a few feet away, smiling with kind eyes, wearing the green sweater she'd bought for him in Kiev. The man she'd loved and married, her dearest friend and her captain—

—*captain. Of the* Vladislav Volkov, *where I am an officer . . .*

It all came flooding back, the terrible, unbelievable things that had happened to them. The transmission from the MIR. The screaming, the hiding, running through corridors that had become shadowed by an evil intelligence—Alexi separated from her when the typhoon had hit and the dreadful, numbing loneliness that had followed as she'd waited for him. The Americans who had come aboard, who had found her husband, horribly transformed—

"Why are you crying, Nadia?"

He was whole again, here in this place. His short hair was clean and swept back from his high, clear brow; his voice was the melodic rumble that she had thought she'd never hear again, the sound of it a soothing balm to her frayed nerves.

"You are dead, Alexi," she whispered, tears coursing down her face. And she realized suddenly what that meant, what it had to mean.

The thought filled her with an intense, sweeping relief.

Alexi shook his head, still smiling. "You are alive, but time is short; endgame. Do what must be done, my brave girl . . ."

He was fading, his body becoming transparent,

disappearing before her wide and desperate eyes. She struggled to go to him, but her legs wouldn't move in this dream reality. She didn't want to be alone, didn't want to fight anymore without him . . .

Nadia! Nadia, wake up!

"Do what must be done," Alexi whispered again, and then he was gone. The pain she felt transcended emotions, crept from her heart to her head and centered in her right temple, throbbing in time to her shaking body—

"Nadia, are you okay? You gotta wake up! Ah, *shit*."

The shaking was a warm hand on her shoulder, the words English. Nadia opened her wet eyes and saw Steve, intense, blood smeared across his face—and the rest of her memory clicked into place as she breathed in stinging fumes, saw the grates of the catwalk around them in the murky light from above.

The detonator. Fuel oil. The intelligence had taken a new form and knocked Steve out, she had been pushed into an open hatch over the hold, hit her head.

"How long?" Nadia managed.

"Eleven minutes left."

"Foster?"

Urgency flashed in his dark eyes. "It took her. I heard it, heard her scream."

The pain in his voice, the loneliness.

"We must hurry," said Nadia, and Steve blew out sharply, reached down, and helped her to her feet.

"The thermite—" he started, but she shook her head. If the intelligence killed them, there'd be no one to reactivate the timer.

He handed her one of the semiautomatics and then they were climbing, Nadia wiping at her eyes from the dream of her dead husband—and praying that they weren't too late to save Foster from a fate as horrible as his.

■ ■ ■

Foster opened her eyes blearily, forced into consciousness by the screaming ache in her arms and shoulders. Her first realization was that she was alive. The second was that she was suspended from her wrists, hung from an overhead pipe in the back of a shadowy room. And the third was that she was in some very deep shit indeed.

There was an electrical cable affixed to her forehead, leading to a computer console next to her. The monitor was blank, but the ones next to it weren't. Goliath was in front of them, standing perfectly still as information flashed across the screens.

Foster stared at the glowing screens for a moment and then closed her eyes, searching herself for a strength that she wasn't sure she had. One screen had shown a layout of the human nervous system; the data on the other was mostly text, but she'd seen multiple diagrams of various parts of the brain.

She tried to find the voice of her father, tried to hope that Steve was still alive, that he and Nadia had made it off the ship—but the best she could do was a desolate wish that the *Volkov* would blow soon and put an end to her miserable fear . . .

Goliath moved and Foster opened her eyes, watched the monstrosity step towards her. She could smell the decay of human tissue beneath the heavy odor of fuel oil, see the bloodless tears in the flesh that stretched across its limbs and body. There was an instrument panel set into the peeling skin just below its massive, insectile head and she saw something emerge from the panel, unfolding.

A spindly metal hand extended and took hold of her face, cold, rounded fingers pressing into her skin.

Goliath's rumbling, mechanical voice emerged from a speaker in its chest. It asked her something in Russian, the tone soulless and deep. It waited a moment and then spoke again.

"Do you speak English?"

Foster stared at it. "Fuck you."

Goliath didn't seem to take offense. "English. Where is the detonator?"

"I forgot."

The metal hand pulled her face closer and the eye lenses of the creature focused on her, glowing faintly with a strange light. The mandibles that were set into the lower portion of Goliath's face started to shimmer with a crackling blue energy, and Foster realized that they weren't mandibles at all; some kind of power conductor—

Huge blue electrical arcs snapped into her face and Foster screamed, the sounds ripped from deep inside as the world turned brilliant and hot, hotter, intensifying. Every part of her spasmed and convulsed in the blue fire and she was dying, it was killing her—

—and it stopped suddenly. Foster collapsed against her binds, her entire body throbbing, .each separate muscle an agony unto itself. Her face was still held by the metal fingers and an-

other tool extended outward, a shining probe
that moved into position directly in front of her
right eye.

"The detonator. Where is it?"

She struggled to turn her face away, wanting
to tell him, it, the thing that had killed her, before it made the pain come again. She couldn't
think straight and it hurt so terribly—

—*pleaseplease don't*—

Foster closed her eyes, the only denial she
could manage, and there was another blinding
flash of trauma, of death, of sickness—

—and her own screams chased her into a gray
place where all thought was lost.

■ ■ ■

They heard the screams as soon as they stepped
out of the fuel bay. Steve sprinted towards the
sound, down a tilting corridor with Nadia close
behind.

The screams stopped suddenly as they
rounded a corner in the dark maze of the deck
and Steve wheeled around frantically, straining
to hear a noise, some sign that she was still alive.
The anguish in her cries had been terrible,
threatened to drive him insane with a kind of
fear he'd never known before—but the silence
was worse, so much worse . . .

. . . *Don't let her be dead, I'll do anything, just
please don't let her be dead*—

From somewhere farther down the corridor,
Foster shrieked and Steve was running again
even as the horrible sound reached them. It fell
away after only a few seconds, but the open
hatch was in sight, not twenty feet away—

Nadia stopped him before he charged in, laid a hand across his quivering arm and shook her head.

Steve paused, took a deep breath, and then nodded. Running in blind would kill them. As it was, the small-caliber weapons would probably be more effective if they threw them at the giant—

—and after this clip, that's all that's left.

They stepped into the room and froze, taking in the terrible scene. The creature stood at a computer console in the back of an empty workshop, perfectly still. Foster dangled by her wrists from a pipe nearby, her head down, her body swaying. A thin cable led from her drooping head to the console where the creature stood. She was alive; he could hear soft moans escaping with each ragged breath, and he thanked God for the pitiful sounds as he moved closer to the fixated machine.

Deep in the giant's midsection was a glowing blue fire, the same blue as the electrical currents that snapped across its body—and, Steve realized, a lot like the blue jelly that had coated Everton's brain.

Gotta be the energy source. It's our only chance.

Steve motioned towards it, and Nadia nodded slowly, her own weapon raised.

He approached the creature as quietly as possible, but the giant gave no sign that it was aware of anything except for the computer screen in front of it. Garbled sounds came from the unit as he edged forward—

—and stopped. *He* was talking, his own voice coming out from the console's speaker.

"I gave us fifteen minutes."

A second later, Nadia spoke. "Checkmate."

He could see the screen now, saw a strange, distorted image of himself and Nadia in their life jackets—and he realized that the replayed scene was from Foster's point of view. The creature had somehow tapped into her mind, stolen a piece of her memory . . . and now it knew where the detonator was.

"That'll be enough of that," he snarled, and jabbed the barrel of the small pistol into the glow of the blue fire.

He emptied the clip. Ten rounds cracked into the mass, sent squealing branches of blue light licking up the belly of the massive creature—

—but that was all. The giant reeled around, undamaged, and swung at him.

Steve leapt away and the enormous fist struck only air. He tripped on a workbench and went down, scrabbling backwards as the beast rotated its upper body completely around, drew to its full height, and emitted a deafening electronic screech. It took one step forward. One more, it would be on top of him—

Bam! Bam!

Nadia fired, the bullets bouncing uselessly off of the plated metal of the creature. She fired anyway, buying time. The monster spun towards her and Steve jumped up, searching wildly for something to use against it as it advanced on the woman. There was nothing, nothing that would make any difference—

—and the dry click of Nadia's empty weapon cinched it. They were dead, the creature would slaughter them and disable the explosive with minutes to spare; it was all over . . .

And that was when a fireball exploded through the room and slammed into the chest of the monstrosity, knocking it down in a shower of fiery sparks.

· 26 ·

Foster dragged herself out of the pain and saw the fireball slam into Goliath. Pieces of skin, bone, and metal flew across the room as the mammoth creature crashed to the deck, as a shadowy man stepped out of the corridor and into the glow of the room, backlit by fire.

Foster opened her eyes wider, trying to clear her head. It was Richie, a grenade launcher in hand. She'd heard gunfire before, heard Steve's voice, but she hadn't been able to wake up.

Steve and Nadia were both in the room, alive, staring at Richie. Foster fought against the gray waves of dizziness that threatened to overwhelm her again, felt astonishment take over as she realized that Richie had come back. He tossed a knife to Nadia and motioned towards Foster, his voice strong and cool.

"Cut her down."

Not so crazy after all ...

Nadia moved towards her and clambered up on a console, started sawing at the cords that held her up, one arm around Foster's waist. Foster stared at the fallen Goliath, crumpled against a support beam across the room. Richie stepped past it and helped Steve to his feet, talking fast.

"Let's get outta here, man."

Foster's right arm came loose and she held on to the pipe, letting the simple ache of her strained muscles drive away the last of the gray as Nadia cut through the second cord and pulled away the cable. The other woman supported her as she slid to the floor and lowered her arms slowly, wincing. Angry red welts encircled both wrists and she leaned against Nadia, shaking, looking up—

—to see Goliath rise smoothly and grab the steel bracing support for the ceiling above the two men, its armature smoking and sparking.

Even as she opened her mouth to scream, the monster tore the brace away violently and slammed one mammoth arm into the decking.

Steve and Richie turned, Richie raising the grenade launcher as Steve ducked—

—and a ton of steel piping and debris crashed down over them. Dust billowed out and rubble spun across the room as Nadia tightened her grip around Foster, kept her from lunging towards them.

"Steve! Richie!" Foster struggled, but Nadia was stronger than she was.

"They're dead, there's nothing we can do!" Nadia shouted. She pulled Foster to the door and Goliath was turning, rotating its torn and crackling body away from the huge pile of wreckage—

The two women ran and Goliath started after them through the dark.

■ ■ ■

Nadia kept a firm grip on Foster's arm as they dashed through the corridor, her thoughts racing, Foster stumbling, obviously in shock from pain and the loss of her friends.

Seven, maybe eight minutes left, keep the creature running, find a way out.

It was impossible, there wasn't enough time—but there wasn't any alternative, either. Nadia pulled Foster along towards the stern, praying that the intelligence hadn't welded any more doors; there were storage rooms ahead, maybe they could find more weapons.

The mammoth creature squealed behind them, close, the pound of its giant legs echoing through the darkness as the *Volkov* heaved against the rumbling storm.

They came to a bulkhead hatch and Nadia pushed Foster through and followed closely, her heart pounding. Together they slammed the watertight door and Nadia spun the hatch wheel. Through the inset window they could see the monster's crashing blue energy, hear the furious electrical screeching of the intelligence inside as it stomped towards them.

The door wouldn't hold out for more than a few seconds. Nadia grabbed Foster's arm and they ran, Nadia trying to remember the layout—

—*the locker!*

Instead of continuing forward, Nadia stopped

at the second hatch they passed and yanked it
open. They scrambled through and Foster spun
the hatch wheel.

There!

It was at the end of the smaller corridor; Nadia
ran for it, pulling Foster, praying that something
had been left behind by the deserting crewmen—
and that the creature had lost them, at least for
a few minutes.

She jerked open the hatch and they fell inside,
panting. A single flickering bulb in the corner
illuminated the tight compartment. Foster collapsed against the door as Nadia hurried to a
cabinet and flung it open.

Relief crashed through her at the sight of the
bright orange suits that hung from the rack. And
behind them, a thick-barreled gun and three
loads in a mounted case.

"Survival suits and a flare gun—Foster, we
have a chance!"

A chance—but very little time . . .

She snatched up two of the heavily insulated
jumpsuits and shoved one at Foster, who took it
numbly, her face pale. For a moment Foster only
stared at it, eyes shocked, unseeing—and then
she dropped it on the deck and started to un-
dress, pulling her stained fuchsia shirt over her
head.

Nadia stripped off her wet sweatshirt and
tossed it aside—then scooped up the tags that
hung from her neck and touched them, felt a
rueful smile tug at the corners of her mouth. Foster was losing her spirit, she could see it in the
other woman's eyes . . .

She took off the tags and held them out to
Foster as the woman zipped up her suit.

"Alexi's ID tags," she said softly. "They brought me good luck."

Foster took them, seemed to focus on them, her gaze sharpening back into reality. She nodded her thanks and Nadia turned away, climbing quickly into the suit and thinking about what Alexi had said to her in her unconscious dream.

Endgame—and she wouldn't leave until she could be sure that her opponent had truly lost.

■ ■ ■

The workbench had been crushed beneath the hundreds of pounds of steel, but the braced legs had only buckled. Steve had missed a broken skull by about a quarter of an inch.

He clawed through the sharp, cold edges of the shattered decking, feeling blood trickle from over a dozen stinging wounds in his back and legs. He could feel a sharp pain in his left side, knew from experience that he'd broken a rib or two—but his injuries were minimal, considering. He struggled into the settling dust of the empty room, choking.

"Richie? Richie—!"

He saw Richie's unmoving legs sticking out from beneath the pile of debris and his heart sank. He crawled over and started to clear away the rubble frantically, pushing at the chunks of decking as fast as he could manage. The creature had gone after the women, the detonator might still be ticking down—

—and this man may have died to help us; I have to be sure.

He pushed away a plank of light metal and

Richie blinked up at him—bleeding but alive. Steve grinned, pulled at his shoulders to free him from the last of the debris—and stopped, staring.

A steel pipe jutted up from Richie's chest, at least an inch in diameter. Steve reached under him gently and touched warm, sticky metal; Richie had been impaled. He wouldn't, *couldn't* survive.

He met Richie's gaze, saw the question there—and shook his head, unable to lie to him.

"We all thought you deserted us," Steve said softly.

"Shows you how smart I am," Richie whispered. His voice was thick with blood. As he spoke, trickles of it coursed out of his mouth, but he struggled to say more, his eyes glassy with pain.

"I'm not such a bad guy," he said weakly.

Steve shook his head, forced himself to smile. "No, Richie. You came back for us, you did good."

Richie's return smile was dreamy and sweet, and Steve felt a lump knot in his throat; it was almost over.

"Steve, there's a . . . way off this ship. Get to the missile room."

"Missile room?"

"C deck . . . and, Steve . . . kill that fuckin' thing."

Richie gasped once more, staring into Steve's eyes—and died.

Steve reached out and shut Richie's eyelids with one shaking hand, then stood up, forcing back tears; there was no time to mourn.

He backed away, took a deep breath—then

turned and started to run, one hand pressed against his left side. He had to try and find Foster and Nadia before the creature did—and he had less than five minutes now to do it.

· 27 ·

Nadia led them running through a labyrinth of corridors that she said would take them back to the filter bay. Foster could feel the seconds ticking away as they hurried through the dark.

"The ship's going to go any second! Nadia, we've done all we can—"

"I've got to be sure!"

Foster knew she was right, but the thought of seeing Goliath again filled her with a terror so great that she couldn't think straight. She hurt, body and soul, so deeply miserable and aching and afraid that it was all she could do to keep going. Not because of some brave, selfless desire to sacrifice herself for the good of humanity, she didn't give a shit about the rest of the world any-more—she just knew that if she stopped, she'd collapse.

And then all of this would mean nothing, they all would have died for nothing, and I can't let that happen . . .

They cut through a small storage compartment that was partly lit and Nadia slowed, looked around the room thoughtfully. Racks of tall, cylindrical metal tanks lined both walls, and although they were marked with Russian letters, Foster figured the *Volkov* probably had all the basics—oxygen, nitrogen, acetylene, others with science-specific purpose. She could see what Nadia was thinking, but they didn't have another detonator; it was too late.

They stepped through a double hatch and into a connecting hall that was too dark to see—and both women froze as the dizzying fumes washed over them, the chemical scent of acetylene gas. Foster reached out towards the wall and felt the cold metal of a pressurized canister beneath her fingertips. They could hear it now, the soft clink of metal ahead and the low hiss of escaping gas. It was a storage corridor—and one or more of the tanks had broken loose.

Nadia reached back and took her arm, urging her forward. Foster tried to breathe shallowly as they edged through the darkness, the heavy etherlike smell making her queasy and light-headed.

"There is a hatch somewhere to the left . . ." Nadia said.

Lights suddenly snapped on in front of them, illuminated the tank-lined corridor with a necrotic blue glow. Foster saw the loose canisters rolling on the deck, the closed hatch a few feet behind them—

—and the source of the light, towering in the

sickly gloom not twenty feet ahead. Foster wanted to scream, to run, but her body had seized, her heart no longer seemed to beat from the absolute dread that enveloped her.

Goliath had been waiting for them.

■ ■ ■

Nadia stared at the creature, shocked.

How did it—

The cameras. She'd forgotten.

The monstrous beast clomped forward through the hissing corridor and she saw that it had repaired itself, that the damage from the explosive grenade had been patched over clumsily with uneven tatters of rotting human tissue. There were no sparks, no flashes of electricity that could set off the streaming gas.

A confused, terrified whisper from behind. "Nadia—?"

Nadia didn't answer, didn't move as she realized what the intelligence held in one giant hydraulic fist. It moved closer and she could smell the sphacelation of its human parts beneath the reek of gas—but still she couldn't move.

The low red light of the detonator blinked from between the skeletal fingers.

The creature clanked to a halt two meters in front of them and raised the hand with the detonator. Nadia could see that it was still counting down, that the numbers had fallen away to less than ten. Without the thermite grenade, it was useless, but she realized that the intelligence knew that; it had detached the timer for another reason entirely.

To show us that it has won.

The hydraulic fingers squeezed and the device crumbled into powder. A deep mechanical voice rumbled out from the creature's chest as the crushed plastic and wire dropped to the deck.

"Checkmate."

They backed away, Nadia reeling from the absolute malice of the entity that had taken the *Volkov*. Murder and dismemberment were not enough, it had to taunt them, terrorize its victims on some kind of sociopathic impulse, and she was afraid, so afraid—

Do what must be done.

She heard the voice of her husband, soft yet urgent in the darkness of her terror—

—and her mind cleared, the exhaustion and horror falling away in an instant. The means to the end were in front of her and she embraced the knowledge openly, free from the despair that had haunted her for so long. She knew exactly what to do. What must be done.

Nadia turned to Foster, to the brave and struggling woman beside her, and spoke quickly.

"Get to the upper deck and get off this ship. You will be the only witness; you have to survive and tell the world what has happened here."

Nadia pushed open the access hatch and shoved the bewildered woman through before she could resist. Foster fell into the other corridor, landed hard on the decking of the lower hallway a meter beneath the storage tunnel.

"No, Nadia—!"

Nadia turned and the creature had moved, stood in front of her, and suddenly it locked one massive talon around her shoulder, crushing skin and muscle. It lifted her easily, held her up in front of its terrible head. She was blinded from the beams of light that fixed across her face, heard the whirring of lenses and the pulse of circuitry beneath the armored limb.

"Are there more of these devices aboard this ship?"

Nadia dug her free arm into the pouch of the survival suit, ignoring the pain as the metal fingers tightened.

She pulled out the flare gun and aimed as best she could for the hissing tanks on the floor behind the creature.

"Nadia, NO!"

"This is for Alexi," she whispered.

She pulled the trigger and welcomed the light.

· 28 ·

Foster ran through the smoking dark, stumbling down corridors that she didn't recognize, lost and not caring that she was lost. All that mattered was that she keep running, away from the brilliant flash of light and sound that she couldn't seem to escape.

Her lungs burned and eyes teared from the heavy chemical smoke that filled the passages. Again and again she ran up against walls and hatches, the pain of impact only reinforcing her need to keep moving.

... no no no ...

When she banged into a bulkhead hatch hard enough to knock her down, she realized that she couldn't run anymore. She staggered to her feet and opened the door, blinking at the dim light in relieved shock. A small cargo bay, empty. Safe. She went through the hatch and sealed it against the smoke and the darkness, gasping the clean air of the shadowy room as she crumpled to the deck.

For a long time she sat with her eyes closed, dirt and sweat coursing down her face as she took huge, shuddering breaths, thinking nothing at all. There was only feeling—cool air and a pounding heart and the echoing sounds of her harsh breathing in the stillness. The pain seeped back as her heart slowed, the leaden ache of her muscles, the bruises and cuts that seemed to cover every inch of her.

With the awareness of her body, she realized that there was something clenched in her right hand. Foster opened her eyes dully and looked down at her fist, uncurling her numb fingers.

Alexi's dog tags and a piece of broken chain. Foster stared at the shining metal for a moment and then started to cry helplessly, softly.

Woods and Everton, Hiko, Richie, Steve, and his partner, Squeaky; Nadia and her husband and probably the entire crew of the Russian ship. They were all dead because an alien intelligence had decided that they didn't belong here—and it all *had* been for nothing, it was a senseless rendering of human lives by a thing that had mistaken them for a glitch, a bug in the machine. A virus.

She wept with the desolation of total aloneness, low, keening cries of pathetic sorrow; why had *she* survived, how was it fair that she was the one to make it? Nadia had sacrificed herself to save the whole goddamn world while Foster had cowered in fear and misery, too terrified to think of anybody else—

Boom. Boom. Boom.

The sound of thundering footsteps vibrated through the empty bay.

Foster raised her head in stunned disbelief—and heard a high-pitched electronic shriek peal through the corridors, from somewhere not far away.

She jumped up, shaking, her heart pounding in renewed terror. It couldn't be, *couldn't*—

Boom. Boom.

Foster turned and ran for a hatch across the bay, past empty boxes and shelves towards a way out. It wouldn't die, there was nothing that could stop it, and she had to get off the ship, had to find help.

She fumbled at the latch, moaning. The door opened and she stumbled through—

—and smashed into a shadowy figure that stood in front of her. Foster screamed and collapsed, sobbing, and then warm arms slipped around her and held her tight in the rocking darkness.

■ ■ ■

Thank God, thank God—

Steve knelt on the deck, holding Foster, unable to believe that she was still alive. He'd heard the explosions and had run frantically through the corridors towards the blast—until he'd been forced to retreat by the toxic smoke. When he'd heard the pounding steps of the creature, he'd had no choice but to assume the worst, had started searching grimly for a way to the missile room, midship starboard—and had found the scuttle just outside of the bay that she'd come from. In another few seconds he would have been gone.

—I got you, never let you go, never—

He held on to her for a long moment, wanting nothing more than to stay there, feeling her in his arms—but the booming steps still resonated. They had to go.

Foster shuddered, clutching him weakly. He pulled back, studied her tear-streaked face, and decided that she was beautiful.

"Nadia?" he asked softly.

She shook her head, fresh tears coursing down her smudged cheeks.

"Richie's dead—"

Another of the creature's eerie electronic squeals cut him off; it was closer than before.

"C'mon, we're gonna get out of here." He started to rise, wincing at the pain in his side—

—and Foster shook her head again, still holding on to his arm.

"I can't," she whispered, and he crouched down again and saw how it was with her; there was a look of utter hopelessness in her streaming gaze, of total despair.

"I can't do it, I *can't*—"

Steve cupped his hands around her pale face and stared deeply into her frightened eyes.

"Yes, you can. And I'm not leaving you here alone. Now, get up, we have to *go*."

For a second he was afraid that he hadn't gotten through—and then she took a deep breath and nodded. They helped each other up, still half embracing awkwardly, and Steve realized that he couldn't hear the crashing steps anymore. He listened for some sound, any hint as to where the giant biomechanoid could be—

—and the wall of the empty cargo bay buckled inward with a deafening *crunch*. Metal wrenched and groaned, the awful shriek of the monster blasting through the empty chamber.

Steve caught just a glimpse of the enormous thing behind the billows of dark smoke that poured into the bay, blackened metal and wire that crawled with a furious blue light. One of its misshapen arms was torn completely away, tangles of circuitry sizzling and snapping from the blighted socket.

Steve jerked open the hatch to the scuttle and pushed Foster ahead of him as the creature shrieked again in maniacal rage, tearing great chunks of metal away in a desperate frenzy to get at them.

He climbed in after her, praying that he was right about this being the passage to the missile room—and that whatever Richie had seen there would deliver them from the *Volkov* and the murderous giant that wanted them dead.

· 29 ·

They crawled out of the scuttle and into the quiet dark of a huge room, Foster holding the hatch open as Steve climbed out behind her. All he'd said on the way up was that they had to get to the missile room, but not why—and she didn't care, as long as he was with her. She was still afraid, but at least she wasn't alone—and it made all the difference in the world.

They edged quickly towards one wall and Steve found a worktable with a light. He snapped on the small fluorescent and both of them turned—and stared wide-eyed at the organized stacks of metal and wire that littered the shadowy deck. There was a faint, lingering trace of pot in the air. Foster almost smiled.

Richie.

One side of the bay was lined with racks of tools and dead computer consoles while the hull

wall was set up with a launch track and tubes—
but it seemed that Richie had sat on the floor to
do his work, and he'd been busy. Foster saw piles
of rivets and bolts, curved pieces of painted
metal, rounded caps and tiny components and
snarls of wire and cord.

But what was he doing *here?*

Steve checked the bulkhead hatches and then
they both walked towards the hull, their boots
clanking across thick metal grates set into the
deck. There was a huge coil of cable near the
launch track, next to a large stack of darkly
cased metallic objects, a duct-taped cluster sitting on top.

Foster blew out sharply. She didn't recognize
everything in the heaped pile, but those were definitely grenades beneath the gray tape.

"Foster, look at this."

Steve was crouched by the track, frowning
down at a bulky mechanical block, covered with
switches and caps.

"What?"

He stood up, still frowning. "It's a rocket motor . . ."

They stepped around to the front of the track
and saw what Richie had apparently been working on. At the base of a massive, open tube was
a platform with a chair welded to it. Straps hung
from the seat, and more loops of cable ran from
the inside rail to the small platform. There was
a bundled pack at the back of the braced stand
that Foster realized was a parachute.

He picked up a makeshift control box, its cable wired through a small hole in the platform.
"Looks like Richie rigged some kind of ejector
seat."

There was a sound, somewhere below—a crash of metal that echoed up through the grating on the deck.

Steve turned to her, his face bruised and pale in the dim light.

"Get in."

Foster looked back at the bizarre contraption and shook her head. "You're crazy. We'd never survive."

"You got a better idea?"

Steve wasn't wearing a survival suit and his life jacket was in shreds; jumping from the top deck wasn't an option, not for him—and she wouldn't leave him, no matter what.

There was another crash, louder this time, and Foster's stomach knotted. She'd thought that she was too drained for terror to take hold again, but she was wrong.

There's got to be another way—
BOOM!

It was the sound of a metal door ripped open directly below them, slammed against steel hard enough to jar the deck beneath their feet.

Blue light shined up through the grating, accompanied by the stink of burnt flesh and melted wire.

Goliath had come.

■ ■ ■

They'd run out of time. Steve grabbed her arm and pushed her towards the platform.

"Get in!"

"No!"

"I said *get in*—"

She searched his gaze with her own, seemed

to accept that there was no alternative.

"I'm not going without you," she said firmly, and Steve realized that he would have to force the issue.

He grabbed both her arms and lifted her onto the platform, broken ribs digging into his side as she struggled against him. He pushed her against the chair and she sat down, hard. He kept one arm across her chest as he fumbled for the straps, managing to pull one of them across her stomach as she pushed at him.

She was strong, but he was stronger. The sound of wrenching metal came up through the grate, pounding and tearing as the creature searched for a way through.

Foster managed to deliver a solid kick to his shin and he leaned over her, looked into the panic and fear and tried to find the right words to make her listen.

"We don't have time! Look, Richie only built this for one, and you're it—you have to go!"

She stopped struggling and their gazes locked, and Steve had so much he wanted to tell her, so many things that he wanted her to know—

The pounding had finally made it to the grate.

Foster leaned forward and then they were kissing, hard, hungry, and surging, the passion sweeping through him like a shock. Every part of him tingled and sang—

—and breaking the kiss was like a physical pain, but he couldn't let her die. He scooped up the control box and stepped away from the chair, filled with too many emotions that he couldn't name.

Two buttons and a toggle switch. He flipped

the switch and a tiny red light appeared over the first button.

Crash!

The floor behind them exploded upwards, the heavy grate ripped aside as two massive steel arms burst into the room, clutching at the shattered deck.

Steve hit the first button and the bay shuddered around them, but the engine didn't fire. The sound of screaming wind blasted through the missile tube as a thick plate of metal rose up behind the rocket motor, a blast deflector shield—

—and the creature clawed into the bay, its huge body tearing away more of the steel flooring as it pushed itself through. Brilliant blue arcs of electricity crackled across its entire body, the cracked lens of one eye oozing murky fluid, its tattered arms reaching out for him as it crawled onto the deck—

—and he leapt onto the platform and thrust the controls at Foster. The monster rose up slowly, would lunge for them at any second—he had to run, try and distract it—

"Push the button and GO!"

Steve turned to jump—

—and couldn't. He looked down, saw that she had hooked a harness strap through his life jacket.

"Not without you!"

The monstrous creature took a single massive step towards them, and Steve grabbed on to the back of the chair, ducked—

—and Foster pushed the button.

▪ 30 ▪

There was a tremendous blast of power as cable uncoiled on the deck of the *Volkov*'s missile bay at an amazing rate. The alien lurched towards the whizzing mass of line and searched its collected data for an explanation; there was none.

It turned towards the multifarious collection that was connected to the end of the cable just as the cable ran out—

—and four trillion kilowatts detonated in the chamber and blew the alien intelligence out of existence.

The explosion ripped through the Russian vessel, the sound of it drowning out the dying typhoon that stretched across the *Volkov*'s path. A hundred feet of the ship's belly was driven deep into the ocean below as more than half of the starboard hull exploded outward, threw red-hot metal and flaming debris hundreds of feet away. A giant fireball mushroomed up into the sky above the ship, the rising flames punching a hole in the tropical storm that held for just under a full minute.

Water boiled and evaporated in the immediate vicinity of the *Volkov*. The ocean surface cratered and pushed out a shock wave of several hundred tons of foaming seawater as the steam rose to join the fire, whiting out the black, swirling clouds of Leiah.

The *Vladislav Volkov* keeled over and sank.

■ ■ ■

Two hours after Foster and Steve landed in a raging sea, the dregs of typhoon Leiah blew past them and revealed a clear and sunny afternoon sky. They held on to each other, Foster trying to warm him with her body as the swells of the gently rocking ocean swept them through an endless plain of murky blue. In spite of her efforts, his teeth chattered violently and he couldn't stop shaking.

They hardly spoke for the next three hours, although both of them smiled when the charred and burnt wreckage started to drift by. And when the drone of the helicopter reached them a short time later, they kissed for the second time.

■ ■ ■

Two burly crew members from the Research Vessel *Norfolk* gently lowered Foster to the deck and onto a stretcher, while two others placed Steve next to her, wrapped tightly in thermal blankets. Foster closed her eyes for a moment, sleepy in spite of the excited voices of the *Norfolk*'s crew and the flurry of activity around them.

"Hey, Foster," Steve said softly.

"Yeah?"

"Thanks."

She turned her head, saw that he was looking at her quite seriously.

"You mean it?"

He reached out and took her hand, staring into her eyes for a long moment. Then he grinned, a boyish smile that lit up his face and made her heart beat faster.

The storm had finally passed.

■ ■ ■

Hiko hobbled out into the sunlight from the bridge of the *Norfolk* and nodded at what he saw. Steve and Foster, holding hands like giddy children. He wasn't all that surprised.

"Need another hand?" he called, and they both looked up, startled.

Hiko grinned. *Oh, to have a camera!*

"Hiko!"

He lurched towards them, still smiling in spite of the awkwardness of trying to keep balanced. His leg was heavily bandaged and the cast on his arm had him lurching around like an old woman. The medic on board said two months, so he supposed he'd get used to it eventually . . .

Foster stood up as he approached and threw her arms around him, hugging him tightly. Hiko grinned down at Steve over her shoulder and then she was standing back, staring at him. He saw that her eyes were wet with tears.

"How did you—?"

Hiko pointed across at the growing pile of wreckage that the *Norfolk* crew had been dragging out of the *moana* all day. The life preserver was still visible beneath a clutter of burnt wood, the legend *Sea Star* inscribed on the side.

Steve shook his head in amazement as Foster sat back down next to him. "You made it!"

Hiko nodded. "I faced my fear. I survived—"

There was a strange, high-pitched squeal from across the deck and all three of them whipped around, Hiko clutching for the *wahaika* that he had carried through the storm—

—and saw the ship's crane lowering the rescue boat onto the deck, the massive arm bending down in a screech of grinding metal.

He looked back at the two of them, saw the same sheepish smile on the *Pakeha* faces that he knew he wore. They were holding hands again.

Foster turned to Steve. "There'll be no machines on that island of yours."

"Or electricity," said Steve, and Hiko shook his head in mock disgust. Love could be a terrible, terrible thing, at least to watch.

Hiko stepped aside as the sailors finally came over to lift the two stretchers and take Steve and Foster down to the sick bay.

Steve called to Hiko as he was picked up, still gripping Foster's hand tightly. "So what *does* your name mean, anyway?"

Hiko grinned. The translation wasn't perfect, but it was close enough.

"Lightning."

The four crewmen carried the two away before he could see their response, but Hiko didn't mind. He hobbled to the railing of the *Norfolk*, feeling tired but at peace as he looked out over the giant sea and felt the sun warm on his skin.

He decided that when the cast came off, he was going to learn how to swim.